"We can stop now if that's what you want."

Antonio rested his hands on either side of her hips but didn't pull back. If he couldn't see her, he at least wanted to be near, wanted to feel her. All his senses were heightened. She'd been driving him wild all day.

"What I want is to be responsible and professional, but apparently I already crossed that line."

Antonio couldn't help but admire her honesty. She wanted him as much as he wanted her. And since they were both adults with the same need, there was no reason for them to ignore this connection.

"I imagine you are always professional and responsible," he countered. "Take what you want, *amante*."

"What does that mean?" she asked.

He leaned forward and whispered against her ear. "Lover."

Her body trembled against his and this moment was even sexier, naughtier, than if they'd been in the light.

* * *

When the Lights Go Out... by Jules Bennett is part of

Dear Reader,

Are you ready for a fun new series? I have been so excited to get these stories to you all! Angel's Share came to me when I visited Castle & Key Distillery in Kentucky. Many of you know I love doing tours of breweries, distilleries and vineyards. Castle & Key happens to not be far from me and I was thrilled to visit such an amazing place. A distillery in a castle? What could be better?

This particular distillery was run by a woman at the time of my tour, though that has changed since. I knew right then that I had to write some kick-ass sheroes with their own castle distillery in the heart of Kentucky! My three best friends are more than ready to take on this man's world.

Up first, Elise Hawthorne. She's my smart, careful, calculated friend. Of course I had to throw in a sexy jet-setting Spaniard to rock her back on her sensible heels. I won't give away too much, but if you like a stranded story, this one is definitely for you!

I hope you enjoy Elise and Antonio's story and follow along for the other friends: Delilah and Sara!

Happy reading,

Jules

JULES BENNETT

WHEN THE LIGHTS GO OUT...

HARLEQUIN

DESIRE

Recycling programs
for this product may
not exist in your area.

ISBN-13: 978-1-335-73573-7

When the Lights Go Out...

Copyright © 2022 by Jules Bennett

All rights reserved. No part of this book may be used or reproduced in any
manner whatsoever without written permission except in the case of brief
quotations embodied in critical articles and reviews.

This is a work of fiction. Names, characters, places and incidents
are either the product of the author's imagination or are used fictitiously.
Any resemblance to actual persons, living or dead, businesses,
companies, events or locales is entirely coincidental.

For questions and comments about the quality of this book,
please contact us at CustomerService@Harlequin.com.

Harlequin Enterprises ULC
22 Adelaide St. West, 41st Floor
Toronto, Ontario M5H 4E3, Canada
www.Harlequin.com

Printed in U.S.A.

USA TODAY bestselling author **Jules Bennett** has published over sixty books and never tires of writing happy endings. Writing strong heroines and alpha heroes is Jules's favorite way to spend her workdays. Jules hosts weekly contests on her Facebook fan page and loves chatting with readers on Twitter, Facebook and via email through her website. Stay up-to-date by signing up for her newsletter at julesbennett.com.

Books by Jules Bennett

Harlequin Desire

The Rancher's Heirs

Twin Secrets
Claimed by the Rancher
Taming the Texan
A Texan for Christmas

Lockwood Lightning

An Unexpected Scandal
Scandalous Reunion
Scandalous Engagement

Angel's Share

When the Lights Go Out...

Visit her Author Profile page at Harlequin.com, or julesbennett.com, for more titles.

You can also find Jules Bennett on Facebook, along with other Harlequin Desire authors, at Facebook.com/harlequindesireauthors!

To my girls.
As you grow into amazing young ladies,
I pray you always take the chance at life and love.
You two are my everything.

One

There could be worse places to visit than an old castle turned into a distillery. The sprawling stone structure nestled among the rolling hills of Benton Springs, Kentucky, and was quite a pleasant surprise. The story behind this structure from centuries ago was rather fascinating...almost as much as the ladies who now owned the place.

Antonio hadn't known what to expect when he'd fired up his private jet and departed Cadaqués, Spain, two days ago, but the beauty of this centuries-old building and lush surroundings reminded him so much of home.

Which was the one place he was trying to break

free from. Well, maybe not the picturesque coastal town itself, but the legacy that loomed in front of him. He had no clue how to break the devastating news to his parents that he would not be taking over the family business they'd created...a family business that should have been handed down to his brother, but tragedy had robbed them all of the future they'd envisioned.

"You must be Antonio Rodriguez."

Antonio turned from admiring the scenic view and nearly stumbled as he took in another stunning sight. The redhead with a wide smile striding toward him was the very woman he'd been corresponding with via email for the past couple of months.

"And you would be Elise Hawthorne," he replied.

He'd not only done his homework on this distillery and the variety of spirits they offered, but he'd also checked out the three dynamic women behind the Angel's Share label.

Elise held the prestigious title of CEO and was the direct contact for all VIP accounts. They'd bounced messages back and forth for some time now and she'd been nothing but professional and accommodating.

Still, nothing had prepared him for that instant punch of arousal to the gut. Who knew tortoiseshell glasses could be sexy?

Elise empowered both brains and beauty...two qualities he found absolutely irresistible, and if he didn't keep his focus on work and his own issues, he'd find himself wrapped up in a tangled mess he didn't have time for.

Shame that. He wouldn't mind getting to know Elise Hawthorne outside of working hours.

She closed the distance between them and extended her hand. "It's a pleasure to finally meet you in person, Mr. Rodriguez."

"Antonio," he insisted, offering her a grin, mainly because he wanted to see her smile in return. He wasn't disappointed.

The photo of the sisters on the company website had been difficult to really hone in on the features of each woman. They all stood in front of the castle and the castle had been the focal point of the image.

But Elise had stood out with that vibrant red hair and in person…she was a damn stunner.

Antonio took her hand and immediately admired the soft, yet firm shake. A powerful woman with confidence and a killer smile…maybe this trip of his to America would be even more enjoyable than he first thought. A little flirting wouldn't hurt anybody.

There was still that fine line, though, and he'd vowed to keep this trip strictly business. This was his last deal before pulling out of the family business for good. He owed this trip to his parents, and he owed it to himself, to push aside his personal wants and focus on the pub side of their restaurants and bringing in new labels never before purchased in their area of the world.

And that was the easy part of the trip. Roaming across the States, going from distillery to vineyard, doing sample tastings and getting to meet new people, was everything that gave him life. He just had no clue, once this trip was over, where he'd ultimately end up.

Grief had him all confused lately, doing more out of guilt and obligation than anything else. Taking over the chain of posh restaurants his parents had started decades ago was not his idea of how he wanted to spend his life. He wanted his own goals, his own dreams…he didn't want to fall into the title that was meant to be shared with his late twin brother. For now, though, Antonio was in charge of upgrading the pub side of each of the family's five restaurants.

If only Paolo hadn't died…

Throughout Antonio's entire life, he'd enjoyed the traveling and experiencing different cultures. He'd never wanted to be in one place and spearhead a dynasty meant for someone else. He thought he could do what his parents wanted and be the son they needed.

He always felt he owed it to Paolo to try. Antonio had put all of his own selfish thoughts and wants aside, thinking he would grow into this role they'd created for him, but that hadn't been the case.

And the longer he let these feelings fester, the more he resented everything about this business. He was going to have to do this last trip and finally have a talk with his parents about the realistic vision he had for his future.

Family was absolutely everything, so how did Antonio break his parents' hearts by walking away from this mega dynasty they'd built? They'd trusted so much to him, hoping to retire soon and leave him in possession of their precious legacy. The last thing he wanted was to be married to a woman…or to a business. He enjoyed his freedoms, always had, and once his brother passed, Antonio realized the importance of living each day like it was your last.

Yet, guilt over being the son who survived had him fulfilling his parents' wishes instead of living his own life.

"Angel's Share is nothing like the photos online," he claimed, refocusing his attention on the breathtaking surroundings. "This is really quite extraordinary and must be seen in person to truly appreciate."

Her smile beamed even wider. Her shy beauty couldn't be denied, but there was something about a powerful, dynamic woman he'd never been able to resist.

Too bad he wasn't here for play. Jet-setting playboy was definitely not the next business venture he wanted to get into.

"Thank you," she replied. "The castle dates back

to the late 1800s. Obviously, there have been some renovations and changes, but the structure remains original. There have been some additions to the out-buildings around one hundred years ago, but those are holding up well, too. We're quite proud of the operation we have and how everything seemed to fall into place for us."

"As you should be."

Elise gestured toward the stony walkway. "It's such a beautiful day. Would you like to start the tour outside around the grounds?"

"I'm at your disposal." He offered a mock bow. "Show me everything you have."

Elise quirked a perfectly arched brow and he realized his words might have come off as offensive, or could definitely be construed a different way.

Instead of saying a word, she merely nodded. He really needed to keep the mood light since they just met. He might have vowed to himself he wouldn't get involved with a woman on this trip, but he hadn't expected to be face-to-face with such temptation and have such a strong urge right out of the gate.

"It's nice to get out of my office once in a while, so we'll start right here." She gestured with her hands out and glanced around the sprawling piece of property. "As I said, the castle dates back well over one hundred years. A Scottish family migrated here in 1845 and took a few years to build this replica like what they'd left behind right down to the drawbridge, which is a fun feature we still love."

As Elise spoke, Antonio tried to focus on her words and the background for Angel's Share Distillery. But there was something so soothing and almost…sultry about her lilt. He always found American women fascinating. They were bold, dynamic, and unapologetic for their ways. Antonio had taken more than one lover here in the States as he'd passed through over the years. This trip, however, was meant for business for his family and for him to possibly explore other business opportunities— something he could do completely on his own.

Unfortunately, there would be no flings while here in Benton Springs. But that didn't mean he had to avoid all temptation.

Elise Hawthorne was definitely someone he wouldn't mind getting to know a little more intimately, and she could certainly make his time here more interesting. Flirtatious smiles and fun banter were still his default mode…it wasn't like he could just turn off who he was.

"What started you in the world of distilling?" he asked as he followed her around the side of the castle.

Elise came to a stop on the path, turning to face him fully. "Oh, well, my sisters and I have always loved this abandoned place. In high school we used to hang out here with our friends and sneak drinks on the weekends and party. Several years ago, when it came up for sale, we all knew we wanted to do something remarkable with it. I guess, in a ridiculous way, you could say we came full circle."

Antonio nodded and chuckled. "That, you did."

"Besides, there's no better location than Kentucky to start a distillery and with this unique setting, we're drawing quite the crowds and business." She beamed as she spoke. "This castle was once a distillery, but when Prohibition shut everything down, they never reopened. A private owner lived here until the late '90s. When he died it stayed empty until we bought it. So, when my sisters and I decided to dive into this man's world, we wanted something more romantic and unique. Since this place was still sitting vacant, we knew we had something special."

"This is definitely unique," he agreed.

"We even have interest in weddings, but we haven't opened up our grounds to that type of venue yet. I guess our romantic angle is working."

Antonio studied her once again, realizing there was something different he kept taking away from her looks. She was quite polished, yet casual, and all business. There were layers to this woman and he wondered just how many he could peel back before his time here was up in a few weeks.

"You mentioned your sisters. When I looked Angel's Share up online, I noticed you all are quite different from each other."

Elise's smile widened and she quirked a brow. "We are very different from our looks to our personalities. But we were raised together. Adopted, actually, when we were only infants. We're closer than any blood relation could have ever made us. I'm the oldest, then Delilah, then Sara. They say I mother them, but I guess that just comes with the territory."

The conviction and love in her tone was definitely something he could appreciate and resemble. A pang of jealousy speared through him, though. Having lost his twin at only thirteen years old from meningitis, Antonio didn't have stories of milestones or accomplishments he could share.

Growing up an only child, losing the bond of a twin, had been life altering for Antonio and had shifted the dynamics with his parents, as well. Now he was the only one they had and that heaviness weighed on him, growing more so with each passing year.

His restlessness and need for freedom started after Paolo's death and he didn't need to pay a psychiatrist to inform him the two were related. He'd needed to get out of the house where so much pain and so many memories were stored, but then after he started traveling he realized he could escape the heartache even if for a short time.

Family meant absolutely everything to him, which was why he'd gone so long with keeping this secret from his parents. Running the chain of restaurants was certainly not his desire. But he couldn't disappoint them and he needed a solid plan of action before he could even entertain the idea of leaving the family business. He didn't want them disappointed, but they deserved to pass their legacy on to someone who would feel just as passionately about it as they did.

"You have certainly created quite a stir in the media and the bourbon circles considering this is typically a male-dominated industry."

Her smile turned to a sneer and he could tell she was fighting back her true thoughts.

"That might be, but we're running circles around them and they can't keep up." She adjusted her glasses and held his gaze. "It's actually been rather enjoyable watching those seasoned veterans try."

Antonio laughed and shook his head. "I meant no disrespect. I'm actually in awe of what you three have done here. Not only have you created the promise of a top-notch bourbon, along with an amazing gin that everyone is talking about, but the world is anxiously awaiting your ten-year bourbon reveal, too."

"Between us, I'm more of a gin girl, so thank you for that." She started walking again down the path, heading toward the back of the castle. "We are really proud of our bourbon and have had tasters from all over the globe come in for samples before we unveil our ten-year. The buzz generated is worthy, I believe. Our products are perfection and I'd put them up against any distillery."

Antonio wished he could have gotten in on that initial elite group, but maybe having this exclusive one-on-one time would prove to be even more beneficial. He wasn't too keen on sharing, especially where intriguing women were concerned.

They reached a back door and Elise typed in a code, then opened and gestured him in. "This may be an old castle, but we have state-of-the-art security. After you."

As soon as he entered, a sense of home overwhelmed him. Antonio couldn't quite put his finger on it, but the old meeting the new really took him back to Cadaqués. He loved his hometown and the rich history with the rolling hills that eased down onto the coast. The old stone paths that led to quaint businesses and homes. His town was not only rich with history, they were also rich with generational families who continued to grow and prosper. Perhaps that was just another draw for him to come to Angel's Share first on his American tour. He could see himself here, as odd and unexpected as that sounded. Other than having a coastline, the similarities were cozy and made him feel welcome.

"I can see why you all love this castle," he told her as she came to stand beside him. "And why you were eager to purchase and find a use for it."

"Oh, you haven't seen anything yet," she beamed. "I'm saving the best for last."

He shifted his attention from the exposed stones and high beams to Elise, who stared back at him. There it was again. That punch of lust he'd gotten when they'd first met. Thinking of the photo he'd seen on their company website, Elise posed with her sisters. She hadn't stood out to him at the time. But now, in person, she pulled him in, captivating him with some invisible power.

"How many tours do you give here?" he asked.

"Oh, we average about ten per day. We like to keep the groups small and intimate so the customers feel like they are getting a VIP treatment. We might be growing fast, but we still want to maintain that small-town, friendly atmosphere."

"No, I mean you specifically."

She blinked, clearly taken aback by his question. "Oh, well, I never give tours. I mean, when we first opened, my sisters and I took turns when we would have one group a day or something like that. Then we started gaining momentum and ultimately hired some younger college kids to do the public group tours. They have vibrant energy and go through a history and spirits training before they can start."

While Antonio was eager to see the rest of this amazing castle and learn all about Angel's Share, he wanted to know more about Elise Hawthorne and what made up this fascinating woman. If he kept asking questions, maybe he'd chisel away the professional exterior and dig deeper into the woman beneath.

He took a step closer, not even realizing he'd done so, but he wasn't sorry.

"The public is missing out on your personality and beauty," he told her. "You are who they would want to see."

She shrugged as if unsure of what to say. Her red hair slid over her shoulder and he wanted to reach out and touch those silky strands.

Oh, man. He was in trouble and he was only on day one of this tour. How the hell was he going to make it staying in this town for weeks?

At least he was only at Angel's Share for this week before moving on to other distilleries in the area. But he'd be in the same town with this temptation for longer than he was comfortable with.

Elise tipped her chin. "Are you trying to flirt with me?"

Antonio couldn't help but laugh. There was that bold American attitude he found so fascinating. "Trying? If you have to ask, maybe I should do a better job."

She quirked a brow, maybe trying to intimidate him, but he only found the gesture sexy. "Is that why you're here? To flirt?"

"I'm here to find the best brands to take back to Cadaqués. I'm here to work my ass off like I always have, and if I just so happen to encounter a captivating, beautiful woman, you can sure as hell bet I will not turn down the opportunity to flirt."

Elise Hawthorne wasn't quite sure what to think of this unflinching, charming visitor, but there was no way to ignore his toe-curling statement...just like there was no way to ignore how sexy and captivating he was. The dark Mediterranean skin, the thick black hair. And the eyes. There was no way to ignore that deep, piercing stare framed with midnight lashes.

And then there was that accent.

Mercy. From the start she'd been trying to focus on being a professional and showing off the work she and her sisters were so proud of. But the man had a thick Spanish accent that only added to his sex appeal.

Sex appeal? How did those words even enter her mind right now? She was too busy to think of having a social life, let alone a sex life. Elise had rearranged weeks' worth of schedules to make this meeting with Antonio Rodriguez. His parents had been famous actors back in the day, and now they owned a wide chain of restaurants across the coast of Spain in tiny towns that were quickly becoming tourist hot spots. And now they could potentially be Angel's Share's first global account. With the Rodriguez name in their repertoire, that would only help to add more accounts across the globe. She needed to land this deal.

Following the Rodriguez family was easy to do, considering they were in the public eye and all over social media. Ignoring all the press that family received would be virtually impossible. Antonio had not only been deemed the golden child, he'd also been given the titles playboy, jet-setter, and wild child.

All of those descriptions were the exact opposite of her and certainly nothing that would make her want to get involved…though she could easily see why he'd become the fantasy of any woman he came in contact with. But she wasn't looking for a man, especially one with such a naughty reputation.

Get your head back in the game, Elise. No more thinking of his bedroom eyes.

Her sisters would absolutely die laughing if they knew Antonio Rodriguez was flirting with her. Of the three girls, Elise was the calmest, the driest, the one who always put work and responsibility over anything else. Sara often called her *boring*. She wasn't wrong, but *boring* got the job done. Elise preferred a nice, tidy world with structure. She didn't like too much shift, and getting infatuated, or anything else, with Antonio, would definitely be a shift.

"Flirting will not get you a discount on any future orders," she told him with a smile, wondering where her own saucy attitude came from. Maybe this banter was contagious. "So you might want to save that for another company you're visiting."

His mouth quirked as if he fought back a grin, but before he could say anything, Sara came through the back door, her hands full of folders, her purse, a laptop case, and her coffee mug, and she nearly dropped everything when she came to a complete stop upon seeing she wasn't alone.

"Oh, sorry," Sara gasped as she blew her hair from her eyes. "I didn't expect to see anyone in here."

Elise welcomed the interruption. She needed a reset to get her thoughts firmly under control. Clearly staying in her office behind the desk day in and day out had clouded her mind. Perhaps she should start doing more tours and interacting with the customers. Then the sexy sight and charming chatter from one charismatic man wouldn't throw her mind into a tailspin.

"No worries," Elise replied. "Actually, I'd like to introduce you to Antonio Rodriguez. You remember me telling you about his arrival."

Sara's eyes widened as she no doubt found Antonio her type. Sara was the one who fell in love easily, who never turned down the chance to let some man charm her. She was always looking for love, but had yet to find the real deal.

"It's a pleasure to meet you," Sara stated with

a grin that only accentuated her dark, wide eyes. "I'm—"

"Don't tell me." Antonio held up his hand. "You're Sara Hawthorne."

Sara attempted to situate everything in her hands and get her chaos back in order.

"Let me help," Antonio offered as he reached out and straightened the pile of folders and adjusted her purse strap on her shoulder. "There."

Sara's red-lipped smile widened as she stared at Antonio from beneath her lashes. "Smart and handy. You are a great man to have around."

Elise had no idea how her very unorganized sister could always look so adorable, sultry, and a hot mess all at the same time, but the woman managed to pull it off.

Elise had seen her sister flirt before, but right now Elise wasn't really finding this cute like usual. Anytime they went out for dinner or just to unwind, Sara was always the one men came to, so it was no surprise that Antonio was returning Sara's very friendly smile.

Sara beamed. "You've done your homework. Have you met Dee yet?"

Antonio's thick, dark brows drew in.

"Our other sister, Delilah," Sara corrected.

"We actually just started our tour," Elise informed her. "I covered a little history of the castle, but we haven't done much else. Antonio only arrived about thirty minutes ago."

"Well, I'm sure you will absolutely love everything about Angel's Share, and Elise is literally the brains behind the operation so you are definitely in good hands."

They all had their special talents and area of skills for the business. Elise was proud of her quirky brain and the random factoids. With an undergraduate degree in History and a master's in Business, she had put her crazy-high IQ to good use and was proud of being known as the "brain" of the group.

She'd never been nearly as stunning as Sara with that flawless skin and glossy dark hair and she certainly couldn't even compare herself to Delilah with her sweet smiles and genuine, natural beauty. Both of her sisters were striking without even trying.

Elise, on the other hand, always tried to find the best pair of glasses to fit her face shape and not make her look like an old lady. She might have a boring lifestyle, but did she have to look the part, as well? Not to mention how she'd just had to make an emergency hair appointment because she'd seen a wiry gray hair this morning and had to pluck the damn thing out with tweezers.

She used to think being so stuck in her ways and not as lively as her sisters was her downfall. But over the years, she'd come to the realization that they were all uniquely different and complemented each other. They each were strong in their own ways and hers just happened to be organization and timeliness.

"I have no doubt I'm in the best hands."

Antonio's comment pulled her back into the moment and she found that midnight gaze locked onto hers. A shiver raced down her spine and she couldn't recall the last time any man elicited such a reaction simply from a stare.

The man was a professional panty-melter and she was too smart to fall into that devious web.

No matter what emotions Antonio pulled from her, Elise knew more than anything else, she wouldn't be bored during this visit.

Elise didn't know if she should be afraid or thrilled.

Two

"And that covers everything we keep open to the public."

Antonio stood at the entrance to the gift shop as customers came and went. He'd seen several groups on tours while he'd walked around the grounds, both inside and out, with Elise. The atmosphere could only be described as electric and the initial tastings had been far beyond his expectations.

"So what questions do you have for me?"

Antonio shifted his attention to her and took a step closer. Her eyes darted to his and he had to give her credit, she kept that professional smile in place. But he'd heard that sweet tone of hers for hours, he'd been enveloped by some fruity perfume, and that striking red hair all pulled back in a low bun only made that sexy, studious side of her even more prevalent. And the way she'd tip her head or adjust her glasses to fully look at him and give her undivided attention had been a hell of a turn-on.

There was something to be said about an intelligent, independent woman who downplayed her beauty or, further still, didn't even recognize the power of it. Antonio wondered if she even realized how stunning she was.

"I only have one question."

She tipped that pointy chin. "And what is that?"

"Join me for dinner this evening."

Her lips pursed as if she was either trying to come up with a reason not to or trying to hide a smile.

"That wasn't a question," she informed him.

"I wasn't giving you an option to say no."

Her eyes widened behind those dark frames. Good. He wanted to keep her on her toes, and a little surprise statement would surely do just that. Although, was she actually surprised that he'd brought up the personal topic? Had he not been forward enough the entire day?

"I don't date," she replied.

And now he was the one who was surprised.

"Ever?"

Elise shrugged a slender shoulder. "I don't give it much thought, actually. I stay pretty busy here."

"Too busy to eat?"

That got a slight snicker from her. "Of course I eat. I have a nice selection of frozen dinners at my house that I can pop in the microwave at any time no matter when I get home. The steak tips with broccoli is calling my name."

"That sounds...well, disgusting and extremely disappointing." No way was he letting that atrocity happen tonight. "Why don't you show me the town and take me to your favorite restaurant, my treat."

Her eyes darted away for a fraction of a second before meeting his once more. "I can't go on a date with you."

But she wanted to...and she was seriously thinking about it, it seemed. Those slight hesitations and the way she looked at him... Yeah, she was giving his invitation some serious consideration.

He didn't know what he was doing or where he thought this would lead, but Elise challenged him with that stoic, guarded demeanor. How could he just ignore that? There was something about her that really made him want to dig deeper, to fully see behind that mask. With the beauty, the intelligence, and the tug of desire, Antonio couldn't just ignore this magnetic pull...even if he'd vowed to behave on this trip.

Oh well. He wouldn't apologize for who he was and there was nothing wrong with being attracted to various women. He'd never made promises he couldn't keep and everyone always knew exactly where he stood. He respected women…he just so happened to enjoy the intimacy, as well.

"Don't call it a date," he told her. "I'm new to Benton Springs and I'd like to see more of the town. You're my tour guide."

She laughed. "For the distillery."

Antonio shrugged and took another step toward her, totally ignoring the people bustling in and out of the gift shop behind him. He only had eyes for one woman right now and he knew he had her just about where he wanted. She was wearing down on her refusal and he had to believe she was just as attracted as he was. Maybe peeling away her layers would be easier than he first thought.

"What's your favorite restaurant?" he asked.

"DiMarco's," she told him without hesitation.

Antonio pulled out his phone, typed in a few things, and had made dinner reservations within minutes.

"All set." He slid the phone back into his pocket. "Dinner is at eight."

Elise blinked as she shook her head. "You just… you got reservations that fast? When I call, I have to wait a week and I graduated with the owner."

"I have a way," he explained with a slight shrug.

"And does that include not taking no for an answer?" she asked, quirking a perfectly arched brow.

"You never came out and said no," he retorted.

"Which means you want to, but you're upset that you want to. Am I right?"

Elise narrowed her eyes. "Are you always this difficult?"

"Difficult? You mean persuasive? Yes, I am."

He waited, letting her mull over whatever thoughts were racing around in her mind. He'd never force a woman to do anything, but this woman was on the fence and all he had to do was wait for her to tip over to his side.

Elise blew out a sigh and threw her hands up. "Fine. I'll go, but it's not you. It's only because I haven't had good manicotti in months."

Antonio laughed. "You're busting my ego over pasta and cheese."

Humor danced behind that solid stare and this was the first time he'd seen that slip of her professional guard. "Your ego needed busting, I'm sure. Pick me up here at seven-thirty. I'll be ready."

Antonio was going to take this win and go with it. "It's a date."

"Not a date. A business meeting."

Antonio leaned in next to her ear and whispered, "I have excellent multitasking skills."

A shiver overcame her, vibrating against him as he had barely brushed against her. He didn't waste any more of her time; he wanted to leave on this note...with her wanting more.

Antonio made his way from the building and

headed toward his rental car. Day one of his business tour and he'd already broken his vow. Oh well. If he was going to backslide, Elise Hawthorne was a hell of a sexy mistake to be making.

Elise stared at the reflection in the old floor-length mirror in her office and applied a pale gloss… which was absolutely absurd. She didn't get fancied up for anybody, let alone a potential customer with too much charisma who likely never heard the word *no*.

Yet, she hadn't been able to say no to him, so here she was in her office, attempting to refresh herself for her not-date.

Why had she agreed again? Oh right. Because he'd asked. Mercy sakes, no wonder he had a reputation. The man was impossible to deny.

Frustrated with herself for being an easy target, Elise removed her glasses and pulled her hair from the bun. She shook out her strands, cursing when her hand got caught in a knot.

"I'm not surprised to find you in your office, but I am surprised to find you fixing your hair."

Elise caught Sara's reflection in the mirror. "Yes, well, I feel like I need to do something a little more fun for my dinner with Antonio."

Not that the word *fun* suited her, but she felt different around Antonio, so why couldn't she alter her look a little?

"Is that right?" Her sister moved on into the office with a smile on her face and eyes wide. "That man is delicious, and that accent…"

Leave it to Sara to adequately put the perfect adjective to their newest VIP customer. Maybe Elise should put Sara on this dinner. She was always looking for love and was determined to find it. Not that Antonio gave off any vibe that he was looking for such things. Quite the opposite, actually.

But the instant the thought of Sara and Antonio out to dinner entered Elise's mind, a sliver of jealousy shot through her…which was absolutely absurd. There was no room for such nonsense and that was not how Elise's mind worked. She was logical, career-oriented, and determined to make Angel's Share the absolute best distillery in the country.

"What are you still doing here?" Elise asked her sister.

Sara stepped into the room and shrugged. "I'm hiding and trying to ignore the fact I need to go to Milly's house."

Milly. Just the name of the sweetest lady who ever lived put a vise around Elise's heart. She missed her mother every single moment of every single day. She'd been gone for a month now and the girls couldn't bring themselves to finish cleaning out their childhood home.

But Milly, a single woman with a heart for love and nurturing, had taken in three little girls from the foster care system and raised them as her own. They'd formed a family that no biological connection could rival.

"Why don't you wait and we can all go together?" Elise asked.

Sara came to stand behind her and Elise caught her sister's gaze in the reflection. There was a pain there that only they could understand. The pain that went so deep from loving someone so much. That was the price of love, though…ultimately, there would be the loss.

"I think I need to go alone just for myself," Sara explained. "If that makes sense."

That made perfect sense. Elise had been to the house alone, but she hadn't bothered anything. That was definitely something they all needed to do together.

"Unless you'd like me to take your place." Sara winked. "Going on a date with a sexy guy with a hot accent sounds like a better plan."

"It's not a date."

Sara lifted a few strands of Elise's hair. "You fussing with all of this says otherwise."

Elise turned to face her sister. "Listen, simply because I don't want to show up looking like I just left work doesn't mean I'm excited for a date."

"I thought it wasn't a date?"

Elise groaned and skirted around her sister. "Go away."

Sara's laughter mocked her, but Elise didn't care. They needed laughter in their lives right now, even at her own expense.

"So tell me the business side of Mr. Rodriguez, because I wasn't around him long enough to get a good vibe other than how hot he was."

Business. Yes. That was what she could focus on, what she had control over. Her emotions...not so much.

"You know Antonio's famous parents."

Sara nodded and Elise went on.

"They are expanding their liquor selection and opening more pub-style restaurants and want to add in some bourbons and gins. We are his first stop and he's checking out a few other distilleries in the area while he's in town. He's also going out west to check out some vineyards. My job is to make the best impression for our distillery because our liquor will speak for itself, and we both know it's the best. We are all in agreement of how important an opening up to the global market will be for us."

"Of course," Sara agreed. "So you did the tour today."

"I did." Elise went to her desk and checked the time on her phone. "We're going to do the secured areas after hours, though. I didn't want to hinder production and I want to be able to devote my attention to his questions or concerns."

"After hours sounds—"

"Professional," Elise stated. "And that's all that's happening. This is no different than any other high-profile customer we cater to and show around from the inside out."

Sara crossed her arms and raised her brows. Elise didn't like this scrutiny, not from Sara. From Delilah, on the other hand, she expected some pushback.

"Except this client is the most attractive one we've ever had and you typically always just stay behind your desk," Sara countered.

Elise squared her shoulders and pulled in a deep breath. "All the more reason to get out and be hands-on. I need the distraction and I need the change of scenery. Besides, I wanted to do the tour, to get back to where I started here. I needed to do this for my sanity."

Sara's features softened as she took a step forward and reached out her hand. Elise took her sister's hand in hers and squeezed.

"I just worry about you and Dee," Sara defended. "It's worse now with Milly gone."

"I get it. I do. We worry about each other and that's okay, but I promise I'm fine. Antonio isn't here for anything other than business and that's all I'm after, too. Getting in with the Rodriguez family in Spain would be a nice feather in our cap."

"I have no doubt you will secure this deal. Just don't fall for his charms," Sara warned. "The media loves to capture him and his arm candy of the week."

Arm candy? Elise nearly laughed at that term being applied to her. She was in a very committed relationship with her desk and her emails. She wasn't looking to change positions anytime soon.

And she sure as hell wasn't looking for love or a fling or anything else other than a hefty order to be shipped overseas for their first global account.

"Well, I'm not looking to be anyone's candy, on their arm or otherwise," Elise assured her sister, then released her hand. "But he is going to be here any minute so I need to get going."

Elise grabbed her purse and slid it over her shoulder. She reached for Sara and pulled her in for a tight, quick embrace.

"Good luck at Milly's," she said as she eased back. "Text me if you need anything. Family comes first."

Sara nodded. "Go on. I'll lock up everything and set the alarms after you're gone."

Elise stepped from her office and headed down the stairs toward the main entrance of the distillery. The wood doors provided no light because they'd wanted to keep as true to the castle and time period it had been built as they could, so Elise would have to step outside to see if he had arrived yet.

As soon as she opened the door, she was greeted with the dark clouds of a spring storm rolling in. Elise pulled her jacket a little tighter around her as her hair whipped around her head. She should have kept it up like she always did.

A large black SUV turned the corner on the road and into the parking lot. The vehicle seemed just as menacing and sexy as the man. A burst of arousal curled through her just as thunder rolled through the ominous sky.

She wasn't into premonitions or anything like that, but she couldn't help but wonder what she was getting into and why she hadn't just let Sara or Delilah take over this account from the start.

Oh right. Because Elise was the VIP account go-to, Sara was their marketing and social media guru, and Delilah was a jack-of-all-trades, filling in where the others couldn't.

Just as the first raindrop hit her face, Elise stepped to the SUV, but Antonio was quick to come around and open her door. He'd changed as well, now wearing dark jeans and a black button-up shirt. Everything about this man intrigued her, fascinated her…and none of that was good. She was in a vulnerable, emotional state. She needed to keep her wits about her tonight.

"You look beautiful," he told her as he assisted her into the vehicle.

Okay. While she didn't want compliments, she was still a woman and she couldn't help those giddy feelings that rushed her. But after a compliment always came that awkward few seconds when she had no clue what to say.

"I like to look my best for manicotti," she joked as she reached for her seat belt.

Just as Antonio opened his mouth, the sky opened up and rain pelted him. He shut the door and raced back around to his side and slid behind the wheel. Once he was in, he turned to face her. Water droplets clung to his dark lashes and Elise hadn't thought it possible for him to get any sexier…she'd been wrong.

"You know how to deflate a man's ego."

He likely meant the statement as a joke, but that husky voice sent a shiver through her. Maybe they should have just stayed at the distillery for their after-hours tour. This dinner, this night, was beginning to feel too much like the date she'd sworn it wasn't.

Three

The storm continued to rage as Antonio drove the windy, two-lane roads back to the distillery. Dinner had been amazing, but the company had been even better. Elise had insisted on paying, which went against everything he'd been taught. But he understood her need for professionalism and control.

Antonio found Elise to be even more fascinating than their initial meeting. She knew her business, that was for damn sure. Clearly, Angel's Share was her passion and her sisters were her life. He could completely understand and appreciate that loyalty to family heritage.

And all eyes were on him, as of late, to carry on his own heritage as the Rodriguez heir.

As he pulled into the parking lot, Antonio pushed aside that crushing guilt that threatened to overcome him. There was nothing he could do about his personal life right this minute, and he wanted to just enjoy the company of a sexy woman who could just be the distraction he needed, but shouldn't have.

"Do you want to be dropped off at the door or at your car?" he asked.

The rain continued to pelt the car and in the distance a flash of lightning lit up the sky. He didn't necessarily want her driving in this storm, but he had no place to tell her what to do and even if he did, she'd likely balk at him for trying to help. Which was just another trait he appreciated with Elise. Some may call it stubborn, but he preferred strong-willed and determined. He lived his life with the exact manner.

Elise glanced out the window, then turned back to face him.

"Are you in a hurry to get anywhere?" she asked.

"Back to the rental house? Not especially. Why?"

She pushed up her glasses and smiled. Damn it, there went that trickle of arousal once again. What was it with this woman? He'd been around and with beautiful women his entire life. Did he only want her because he'd deemed her off-limits? He never did like the word *no*, but this was different. This was his own self-control…which seemed to be dwindling with each passing moment.

"I still owe you an after-hours tour," she told him. "Do you have an early morning tomorrow?"

Even if he did, he wouldn't be turning down her obvious invitation.

"I have the tastings of the exclusive labels you scheduled for one o'clock tomorrow," he informed her. "Then my next tour is in three days, just a couple towns over."

Elise waved her hand. "Well, go ahead and cancel that. No need to waste your time when you've clearly had the best."

He couldn't help where his mind went—to an instant image of Elise completely bare for him, wearing those glasses and nothing else. That long, silky red hair all around her shoulders as she stared up at him and he claimed her as his own.

"I can't resist the best."

Her smile froze as her eyes darted to his lips for a fraction of a second, but that was long enough for him to know this attraction wasn't just one-sided. Oh, she was likely fighting an internal battle just like he was. Good to know because he wasn't sure how long he could hold out on reaching for her. What would one kiss hurt? They were adults and clearly, there was already some instant pull they both felt.

"Are you ready to run for it?" she asked with a wide smile on her face.

Antonio nodded with a naughty, crooked grin. "You seem excited."

She shrugged a slender shoulder. "I love a good thunderstorm and I love showing off what we've done here. Of course I'm excited."

Her enthusiasm was contagious. Not that he was a fan of storms, but he was a fan of Elise's. Somehow in this first day of being in her presence, he'd nearly put aside the anxiety he had, thinking about his parents and his next step once he returned home. How Elise managed to hold his attention so completely was a mystery to him, but one he intended to solve.

"I'll follow you," he told her as he shut off the vehicle. "On three. You ready?"

She nodded and reached for her door handle.

"One, two—"

"Three!" she yelled as she jumped from the car.

Antonio raced after her. The cool rain pelted his back as he hunkered against the harsh winds. In an expert move, Elise had the front door unlocked and open just as he got there. They both stepped inside, instantly away from the harsh elements.

Antonio wiped his feet on the large rug with the Angel's Share emblem embossed on it as Elise punched in a series of buttons on one alarm, and then moved to the second panel and did the same. The doors clicked back to locked and lights flickered on.

"This place can be a bit creepy at night when I'm here alone, especially during a storm." She swiped the droplets from her face, removed her glasses, and pulled her hair over one shoulder. "But I can't think of a better time to show you around. I love the history here."

"I admit the castle drew me in immediately when I saw it online," he told her. "But when I pulled in this morning, I felt like I was home."

She cocked her head aside and reached for the hem of her shirt to clean off her lenses. "How so?"

Antonio pulled a handkerchief from his pocket and offered it instead. Her hand brushed his and he wasn't surprised by another shock of arousal, but he was surprised that something so simple could have him so worked up.

This entire day had been nothing but verbal and emotional foreplay.

"My small town is rich with history," he explained, focusing back on her question. "The castle there dates back a little earlier than this one, and we have some amazing architecture as well in our downtown buildings."

She stood there staring, not taking the cloth he'd offered.

"What?" he asked.

"I'm fascinated about your hometown, but are you going to pretend like it's normal for a man to still carry a handkerchief around?"

Antonio took her glasses and cleaned them for her. "It is normal, at least to me. My parents instilled manners and my father always carries one, so I guess it was just passed down. Silly things, really, but I never thought about it."

"They must be proud of you."

Of course they were, they fully expected him to take over their dynasty. As the only child now, they had silently placed a heavy load on his shoulders that he wished like hell he could off-load on someone else. But he couldn't do that to the people who loved him most.

Antonio didn't reply. He stepped forward, closing the gap between them as he eased her glasses back into place. Her eyes met his, locking him in as he was unable to move, unable to breathe.

Thunder rolled outside the castle walls and part of him wanted to ignore everything but the sexual attraction pushing them together. But this was crazy. He'd only met her this morning and he was only here as a family representative, nothing more.

But there was more. So much more than what he'd initially planned or counted on. He wanted to erase that sliver of space between them and cover her mouth with his. The need consumed him. The need to taste her, to taste the rain on her lips and explore her on a whole new level.

Aside from the fact he had a craving for her like no other, he also desperately needed this distraction. There was no better way to forget his troubles than with the affection and companionship of an intriguing woman.

Elise blinked and cleared her throat as she took a step back, breaking the spellbinding moment. Antonio missed his chance and wished like hell he would've just gone in for it. What would she have done? There wasn't a doubt in his mind she would have reciprocated the kiss, and he had every intention of finding out…soon.

Each time he started to get a little closer, that mask went back in place. One of these times he was going to rip it off and see the true Elise. Damn it, that silent challenge she threw down was likely lost on her, but not him. He welcomed the defiance.

"Are you ready to get started?" she asked, adjusting her glasses back into place.

"I'm at your mercy."

Her lids lowered slightly and the pulse at the base of her neck beat fast. Oh yeah. She wanted that kiss just as much as he did. Between the storm outside and the fact they were alone in an old castle, they had the perfect combination for sexual tension.

His body stirred, his desire soared. And he'd done

all of this to himself. Had he not asked her to dinner, had he not followed her inside moments ago, he could have gone back to his rental where he was sure to keep his hands to himself.

But his needs weren't the only issue. No, the issue was seeing that matching passion in Elise's eyes. The pull was too fast, too strong. He couldn't just ignore how she looked at him…and how she seemed to be struggling just as much as he was.

"Let's start at the beginning," she told him. "We'll go to the mash area, which is that amazing scent you get as soon as you step inside the building. We actually have a candle in our gift shop that mimics the aroma."

When she turned away, Antonio followed those swaying hips. He believed that, for the woman who was all business, there had to be some serious pent-up desire inside there. He wanted to be the one to pull that out. No, he *needed* to be the one.

He couldn't describe the all-consuming yearning to have her, to claim her.

Elise led him up the metal stairs toward the scents of yeast and mash. Even this didn't take away from all of his erotic thoughts and images of Elise. While she was trying to maintain a professional exterior, he knew what was boiling deep inside. Maybe they just met, but he knew women, and he recognized that indescribable need.

All he could think of was that they were alone, with a storm raging outside just as it raged inside. The only thing to stop them from crossing that line from professional to personal was themselves…and he was ready to ignore all the reasons why they shouldn't.

"So Angel's Share is a little different in the way we begin our mash process and that is actually kept a secret even from our exclusive clients."

She flashed him a smile he could only describe as proud.

"Even our most important VIP customers aren't in on that," she went on. "But once you visit other distilleries, you'll notice this aroma is fresh. That's the only way I can describe it. There's a subtle sweet undertone, but nothing that will take away from the rich bourbon flavor."

He listened as she pointed toward pieces of equipment, how she discussed their startup and their struggles. How they borrowed so much and called in every favor to get this place up and running. Which was quite an undertaking since bourbon has to age for years before it's ready for public consumption. They'd been smart in also offering gin to get their name out there until their first bourbons were ready, so by the time their ten-year bottle rolled around, Angel's Share would already be well-known.

Brains and beauty. There was no way this operation would fail.

"We have excellent bourbon and gin right now and as you know, we're unveiling our first ten-year at our anniversary gala." She turned to face him fully and kept that megawatt smile in place as she pushed up her glasses. "If you're still in the area, you are welcome to come."

He'd make sure he was in town, no matter what schedule he had to rearrange to be here.

"So where else are you traveling?" she asked. "I need to know who my competitors are."

"Right now I'm not interested in anyone else. You're top of my priorities."

Elise motioned for him to follow. "In that case, let's keep this tour going so I can secure you're mine."

Oh hell. There wasn't much *securing* that needed to be done. As far as he was concerned, Angel's Share would be going into his family's businesses.

Besides the fact Elise had him under her spell, he had loved the tastings he'd done earlier during the main tour. The richness, the subtle char from the barrels and the hints of nuttiness were perfect and exactly what he was looking for in bourbons. He hadn't come here looking for the gin, but since he'd be doing business anyway, the smart decision would be to incorporate all of Angel's Share's products.

Elise led him back downstairs and down a long, narrow hallway lined with old stone. The thunder continued to rumble outside as he followed Elise down another set of steps. They headed toward a basement he hadn't even known existed. When they came to a steel door, she punched in a code. A series of beeps echoed in the hallway before the latch on the door clicked. Elise pushed through the opening and the creaking noise had Antonio chuckling.

"I feel like this is how a missing person's case would start," he joked. "An old castle, a storm, the dungeon…"

Elise snickered as she gestured for him to enter ahead of her. "I assure you, I'm not kidnapping you. This is the room that is my absolute favorite and we don't let anyone down here. Actually, very few employees even know its existence and the ones who do aren't given the passcodes."

Yet, she'd brought him here. That spoke volumes for how well their connection was already. Elise was the perfect distraction. He'd known coming to the States would help keep him busy and keep his mind off a conversation he wasn't ready to have with his parents. Something was missing in his life and he had no idea what the hell could fill that void.

But diversions by way of intelligent women were most welcome until he could figure out his life.

"So what is this special area?" he asked.

Elise led him down another hallway and to another door. With her hand on the knob, she looked back over her shoulder. "This is where all the history is located."

He followed her inside a room with stone walls. An old desk sat in the corner, a floor-to-ceiling shelf nestled in another corner. There was at least a light overhead, but not much else.

"Are you sure you're not about to lock me in here?" he joked.

Elise went to the shelf and pulled out a book before meeting his gaze.

"Do you want to get locked in here?" she retorted.

"Are you flirting with me?"

Elise pursed her pale pink lips. "No flirting. We're here for work, right?"

He was having a difficult time remembering that, and all of her smiles, her wide eyes behind those glasses, and whatever this magnetic pull was, Antonio knew he couldn't stay alone with her much longer.

She sat the book on the desk and carefully eased the cover open. Closer inspection showed the book was definitely old. The yellowed pages with frayed edges had a cursive writing that was both elegant and scratchy. History had always fascinated him and seeing the delight on Elise's face told him this was just one area they had in common.

Not that he was looking for anyone to bond with on a deeper level. He wasn't so sure long-term commitments were for him. Oh, the whole love and marriage thing worked great for his parents. There was no denying how much they adored each other since the moment they'd met while filming a movie decades ago. And it wasn't that he didn't believe in love. Antonio just didn't think he could commit to one person for the rest of his life. All of that sounded so…permanent.

Exposing his heart to someone with the hopes of forever would only lead to pain and loss. He couldn't take the risk of being that destroyed ever again.

Besides, he enjoyed taking off on a whim and traveling and doing his own thing on his own time. Taking over in a position meant for someone else wasn't fair to him or his parents. Surely, they wanted someone who actually had a passion for the business like they did…and that wasn't him.

Maybe all of those thoughts made him a selfish person, but at least he was honest. And any woman he was with knew exactly where he stood. He might not be looking for commitment, but he did respect women and would never lie about something so serious.

"So what are we diving into?" he asked, standing next to her at the desk.

"This is one of the diaries from the original architect of the castle. We found these when we were restoring this place and we keep them locked away."

"Are you serious? That's amazing."

Antonio glanced at the dates just as the lights flickered for a brief moment and came back.

"We should head back upstairs," Elise told him. "You don't want to be down here if the electricity goes."

She'd barely gotten her sentence out before the lights flickered once more and ultimately gave up, plunging them into darkness.

Antonio waited a beat, hoping the power would return, but no luck.

Elise cursed beneath her breath, turned on her cell flashlight, and left the room. The very unladylike groan from the hallway told him this was not a good predicament they were in if she was this frustrated.

Of course not. So...

"Are we trapped?" he asked.

"For now. You're not claustrophobic, are you?"

Antonio shook his head and then realized she probably couldn't see him.

"I'm not," he told her. "Do you have cell service here?"

She turned her phone over and then held it up, walking all around the room. Antonio pulled his out and did the same...all for naught. They were underground and surrounded by old stone.

"Well, the good news is there is a bathroom down here," she told him with a half-nervous chuckle. "The bad news is nobody will be here until morning."

"That doesn't sound like bad news at all," he retorted. "Sounds like you and I are going to get to know each other even more."

Four

Why did that sound like the most delicious threat ever?

Elise certainly hadn't lured him down here for any shenanigans, but now they were stuck in an old dungeon with very little furniture, no lights, and a hell of a lot of sexual tension.

Of all the sisters, Elise was the least likely to find herself in this position. Delilah was always the mischievous one growing up and Sara would welcome the chance to get stuck during a storm with a sexy man. Nothing about this scenario was like Elise.

Growing up, she had been the studious one, the by-the-book one. She'd been the one to make her sisters stay the course and see their dreams come to fruition even when things seemed impossible.

And perhaps that was why she was so damn enthralled and almost excited that she was locked in a castle basement with a sexy Spaniard. Things like this never, ever happened to her.

"I have to apologize." Talk about unprofessional and embarrassing. "When I wanted to give you a tour, this wasn't exactly how I expected things to go."

"Things happen. Even you can't control Mother Nature."

His low voice with a thick accent washed over her in the darkness—the man might as well have reached out and touched her.

"We have power outages with storms, but they usually don't last long. Maybe we'll be saved before morning."

"Oh, I can think of worse situations. This is just an unexpected moment. Life is full of them."

Elise tapped her phone for some light as she crossed the tiny room and took a seat against the wall.

"Are you always this optimistic?" she asked.

"Not always."

He came and took a seat next to her, his thigh brushing against hers. She'd thought coming over here would make him stay over there. How could she keep resisting?

No, the question should be *why* she thought she had any right to have to resist. This was a business arrangement. Elise wasn't looking to complicate things or do anything with Antonio other than land this important account.

"My parents are all business, all the time." Antonio's statement cut through the darkness. "I couldn't be more opposite and sometimes I wonder if I even belong to them. I mean, if I didn't look exactly like my father, I'd question."

"Delilah, Sara, and I were all adopted by our mom, Milly." Elise found herself remembering all the amazing moments from childhood. "Milly was a saint for taking on three kids all under the age of four and sticking by us no matter our crazy ideas."

"Is she part of the distillery?"

Elise swallowed the lump of grief. Time healed all wounds...or some such saying, but Elise's ache continued to grow with each passing day.

"She actually passed about a month ago," Elise informed him. "But she was a huge part in our success and will always be here in spirit. We definitely wouldn't have gotten anywhere without her."

Antonio's strong hand settled on her thigh, sending way too many emotions shooting through her. He was offering comfort and she was having the total opposite reaction.

"Sorry to hear that. Grief can make you really appreciate family and how much they enrich your life."

The conviction in his tone seemed to just tug her even more toward wanting to know more.

"Sounds like you speak from experience," she commented.

"I have my own loss I deal with, but we don't need to get into that. We're talking about you. I'm sure Milly was proud of you and your sisters."

Elise let the conversation circle back to her. She didn't want to push when he obviously didn't want to talk about his own pain.

"Oh, she was. When we first had the idea of the distillery, she told everyone who would listen. Then, once we bought the building, she brought all the members from her yoga classes to tour the place."

Antonio's rich laughter lay like a warm blanket over her. Elise closed her eyes and rested her head back against the cold wall. She supposed if she ever had to get locked down in a century-old dungeon, being trapped with Antonio was the best way to go. At least she wasn't completely alone because being alone right now with idle time only made her think, and thinking led to grieving and she didn't want to go down that path. Even though weeks had passed, if she started giving in to her thoughts, then she'd have to admit the truth and come to terms with what everyone called "her new normal."

"And did the yoga class end up back here for tastings once you opened?" he asked.

"Of course. Not only that, they had a special yoga

class on the rooftop at sunset once a week that entire first summer." The moment in time rolled through her mind like an old movie. "I like to think our marketing skills really boosted our business, but looking back, it could have been all the grandmotherly types in spandex and posting on social media that amped up the attention."

He chuckled again. "I'm sure that didn't hurt, but you and your sisters have something uniquely special here."

"We're women, I know. We hear that all the time from shocked potential clients who think we're just a front and there's actually no man behind the operation."

"Believe me, I'm well aware there are three brilliant women running Angel's Share," he replied. "All of you being beautiful is just an added bonus."

Antonio's hand remained on her thigh and she wondered if he even realized it. She sure as hell did. The warmth, the strength, emanating from him was not helping her ever-growing desire. Because being stranded here for the time being was oh so helpful.

"Working in an industry typically run by men, there have been some struggles and barriers we didn't expect," she admitted. "But I assure you that if you work with us, you won't find an easier company to partner with and you'll have happy customers back home once you introduce Angel's Share."

He gave her thigh a gentle squeeze...apparently,

he knew all along that hand was still there. She imagined someone as powerful and regimented as Antonio wouldn't miss any detail—especially when it came to women.

"I have no doubt we will work well together or I wouldn't have made the trip halfway across the world to be here."

Now he did slide his hand away, but his body still aligned with hers. Their arms, their hips, their legs. Elise wanted to shift slightly, not that she wanted to get away from him, but the longer she kept feeling his touch, the more she wanted…well, more. No matter how innocent this all seemed to be, there was no way she could deny the undercurrent and she wondered if they were going to get out of here before anything rose to the surface.

"We're not talking work while stuck here," he told her.

"We're not?"

"I want to know more about you as a person, not as a distiller."

Elise blinked against the darkness, wishing she could see his face, to read his expressions and what she saw staring back at her. But if they were going to have such personal conversations, perhaps darkness was her best ally here.

Elise had always kept her emotions close to her heart. She'd always had her inner circle of those whom she trusted and let in. Her sisters had cared for her like no one else.

Except Milly. Milly had cared.

"I'm a pretty boring person. If you want excitement, that's Delilah or Sara. Dee is in the process of a divorce, though, so I'm not sure how much fun she'd be. I think the divorce is a mistake, but she didn't ask my opinion, so..."

Silence filled the room, far longer than Elise was comfortable with.

"Her husband is a divorce attorney, so there's some irony there," Elise added, wondering what else she could share that kept them off the topic of the fact they were alone or that there was this crackling tension all around them.

Elise sighed and stretched her legs out before her, crossing her ankles as she continued. "Sara, on the other hand, believes love is going to sweep into her life and whisk her away to some royal fairy tale. We've tried to explain to her that she already owns a castle, it just didn't come with Prince Charming. She seriously dates all the wrong men, but she's not about to give up."

"And what about you?"

"What about me?" she asked, her heart beating faster because now he wanted to zero in.

Antonio shifted, his arm brushed hers a few times and she realized he was rolling up his cuffs on his dress shirt. Mercy sakes, the forearms were coming out. She fell into that category of forearm-loving women—she couldn't help herself. There was something so sexy about those strong muscles that were usually underrated.

"Are you married or divorced?"

"Is that your subtle way of asking if I'm single?"

"I'm not being subtle. I don't play games."

Apparently not, which was just one more layer of appeal she didn't need to notice or find more enchanting.

"I'm single. Never been married, unless you count my office. I'm in a serious relationship with my new cushy leather swivel chair."

Antonio let out a deep sigh as he shifted, his legs rustling against hers. Elise tried to have no reaction whatsoever, but she couldn't help those tingles and happy dances going on inside her. If there had been any question before, there were none now. Antonio Rodriguez was flirting with her and she was absolutely loving it.

"My parents work too hard," he replied. "They say that's so they can leave a legacy to me when they retire. There's so much more to life than working and we've learned that life is definitely too short. Why shouldn't people have fun while working?"

So he'd learned life was too short and he was grieving. He'd definitely lost someone close…but who? If he wanted to reveal or open up, he would, so Elise kept the conversation going and let him have the lead.

"That's a good question," she agreed. "I guess you just have to find what you love in life and then your career doesn't seem like a job. I mean, I definitely put this place and my sisters' needs above my own, but I love what I do and I love seeing everyone around me happy."

"Even at the expense of your own personal life?" he questioned.

Elise shrugged, not thinking he couldn't see her, but he could feel. She grew twitchier sitting here, so she came to her feet and removed her jacket. She didn't know if it was the sexy man or the enclosed room making her hot all of a sudden.

"I'm not sacrificing anything," she defended. "I don't have anything going on in my personal life so there's no reason I can't put everything else first. Maybe once I get all of this on a solid foundation, then I can start assessing my time away from here."

She thought he would stand now that she had, but there was no movement from Antonio. Elise reached her hands out slowly, feeling for the edge of the desk she knew was close by. Once her fingertips hit the curved edge, she turned and eased one hip and then the other up.

There. If she stayed up here, then she wouldn't have to be too close and she wouldn't have to have those "innocent" touches and brushes. Not that she didn't enjoy them…that was the problem. She enjoyed Antonio a little too much and this was only day one of his visit.

She had to start pulling back before she got lost in those thoughts in her head and ended up acting on her sudden desires.

"You're high-strung."

Elise stilled as his accusation wrapped around her. "Excuse me?"

"You're having a difficult time sitting still, you put your sisters and work ahead of everything, and you don't even like to talk about yourself." Now she heard him shifting and knew he'd come to stand. "What do you do for fun?"

"Fun?"

Once again, Antonio's low, rich chuckle penetrated her. It was a laugh, for pity's sake…a laugh at her expense, by the way, and she still found him utterly sexy and irresistible.

"So even the word is a foreign concept," he confirmed. "When you leave work, what's the first thing you do?"

"Take my bra off."

Damn it. That was not what she wanted to come out of her mouth and that sure as hell wasn't what he was asking.

"Fascinating image," he murmured, his feet shuffling across the old stone floor as he came toward her. "And then what?"

Had his voice just taken on a sultry tone? If the power wasn't restored soon, Elise knew she was not going to be able to resist him much longer. How had all of this spiraled so far away from professional and a working relationship to ending up locked in together with an insurmountable attraction?

He was a client, one very prestigious client from another country. This account could open major doors for them and all she could think about was ripping off his clothes and seeing just how sturdy they used to build these old desks.

She circled back to answer his question instead.

"Sometimes I watch historical documentaries or take a bubble bath if it's been a long day."

"Is that right?"

Oh yeah. Definitely more sultry now and he stood much closer. So close, in fact, she could feel his breath on her cheek. Elise closed her eyes as her entire body responded with a flare of arousal she hadn't felt in such a long time.

"I'd say with as hard as you work, you deserve some pampering. Do you ever get a massage?"

"Um...no. I..." *Can't think.* "No massages. I never make time for appointments like that."

His hand smoothed her hair from her shoulder, cupping it just so, then he started kneading. She tipped her head, gladly giving him better access. She should put a stop to all of this, but...why? They were both adults—clearly, he wouldn't be touching her if he didn't want to and she sure as hell wanted him to continue. There was nobody to tell them this was wrong.

So why was she letting those negative thoughts creep in? Just because he was a potential client, one had nothing to do with the other.

Her mind was all over the place, bouncing back and forth on whether she should do what she wanted or stay the course of her usual by-the-book approach. She'd never had to fight against herself before and right now the internal struggle was extremely real.

Then again, she likely couldn't concentrate on any coherent thought when those magical hands were working her over.

"Maybe you're in the wrong industry," she moaned as he went to the other shoulder. "Have you thought about being a masseur?"

"Making a woman feel good would be an excellent way to make money." His warm breath tickled the bare skin along her neck. "I wouldn't be opposed to a career change."

Elise sighed, or maybe she moaned again. Either way, she wasn't ready to call this quits just yet. As long as he was willing to work out her tension, she was going to let him.

"Turn around so I can do this properly."

She stood and turned her back to him. Then he stepped in closer behind her, so close his long, lean torso brushed against her back and she stilled, her breath caught in her throat.

"I can't take much more if you keep moaning like that," he whispered in her ear.

The heavy silence of the room made that seductive whisper seem like a boom. As with everything else she'd learned from Antonio so far, there was a commanding presence that couldn't be ignored or denied.

Elise pulled in a deep breath and slowly turned to face him. Even though it was dark, maybe because it was dark, she wasn't hiding what she wanted any longer. And she wanted to forget that she was the responsible one, the by-the-book one.

She hesitated for a second before she decided to stop overthinking everything in her life. Now was her time, her night, to live in the moment.

"Then do something about it."

She threw down that proverbial gauntlet and waited. She wanted to forget everything outside this room and let Antonio Rodriguez show her exactly what she'd been missing out on.

Five

Antonio cursed himself, wondering if he'd come on too strong or made Elise too uncomfortable by his blatant words and advances. Those were the last things he wanted. He just couldn't seem to get a grasp on his own control, not when the ache and desire were far too strong.

The second she turned, he waited for her to tell him this was a professional relationship only and that all hands and sexual comments should be kept to himself. But it was dark, too dark, and he could only feel her…which was precisely how he got into this predicament to begin with.

Elise's hands fumbled around over his chest, then

flattened as she moved them up and over his shoulders. As much as Antonio demanded control in all situations, this one was quite different and totally new territory. He wanted Elise, there was no denying that truth, but he also wanted her to be comfortable and he didn't want to come across as domineering.

Then her body brushed his from chest to hip as she aligned their bodies, and Antonio came to the realization that relinquishing control could be a very, very good thing.

Her lips brushed along his jaw, then his chin, as she slowly made her way to his mouth.

"We're on the same page, right?" she murmured against his lips.

Oh hell, yes.

Antonio gripped her waist and pressed her even farther into him as he covered her mouth with his. That question was all the green light he needed to act on this attraction. The moment the tip of his tongue touched hers she came alive in his arms. Clearly, her own pent-up desires had been just as fierce and strong as his own.

Her fingertips dug into his shoulders as she opened for him, letting out one of those little moans that had already driven him beyond his breaking point. How could a woman with this much passion hold it all back? She deserved an outlet and Antonio wanted nothing more than for her to use him.

With careful, strategic motions, Antonio turned

them around. He kept one hand on the small of her back, while he felt behind her for the desk. Finally, the edge of the desk grazed his fingertips and he took another step until Elise was against the top. He lifted her, setting her on the solid surface, all while keeping his mouth on hers. He couldn't get enough and he'd just gotten started.

The question was, how far did she want to take this? She'd given no indication he should stop or that she was hesitant, but he also didn't want to assume she was ready for everything he wanted to give her.

Elise spread her legs apart, allowing Antonio to step in farther.

But then she eased away from the kiss just enough for him to still feel that warm breath tickle his face.

"What are we doing?" she panted. "I mean, I know what we're doing, but is this smart?"

Smart? Probably not. But what did common sense have to do with any of this? Sure, he'd told himself he would focus on business and trying to figure out what his own next steps should be to break away from the family legacy. But that was before he'd met Elise, and he couldn't think of a better distraction than this fiery vixen.

Who could blame him? There wasn't a man alive that would turn her away. She was the perfect package, especially because she wasn't looking for more than this, either. Her dedication to her work and family made any type of relationship nonexistent...just how he liked things.

"We can stop now if that's what you want," he told her.

Antonio rested his hands on either side of her hips, but didn't pull back. If he couldn't see her, he at least wanted to be near. He wanted to feel her, to smell her. All of his senses were heightened now that one had been removed. But what he wouldn't give to see this body of hers. She'd been driving him crazy all day with those curvy hips and dip in her waist. While he couldn't wait to get his hands on her bare skin, he did wish he could take her in completely.

"What I want is to be responsible and professional, but apparently, I already crossed that line when I climbed up your body a moment ago."

Antonio couldn't help but admire her honesty. It was that transparency of hers that he found so refreshing and perfect. Too many people who surrounded him were either trying to impress him or they wanted something from him. From everything he could tell, Elise was a genuine person with no ulterior motives other than she wanted him as much as he wanted her. And since they were both adults with the same need, there was no reason for them to ignore this connection.

"I imagine you are always professional and responsible," he countered. "Take what you want, *amante*."

"What does that mean?" she asked.

He leaned forward and whispered against her ear. "Lover."

Her body trembled against his and there was something almost on a whole other level that made this moment even sexier, naughtier, than if they'd been in the light.

"You can be whatever you want here," he assured her. "Anything that happens here, stays between us and has nothing to do with the outside world. Not work or family. Just us."

Elise let out a soft sigh and his body immediately responded. He wanted her, but he had to wait to see where her head was at. No way did he want to coerce her into something she wasn't ready for.

"Just this once, right?" she asked. "And nobody has to know."

"Nobody."

"And this won't get in the way of work?"

He had her. They both knew it…and he hadn't even bothered replying to her *just once* question. Maybe once wouldn't be enough, maybe it would, but he was smart enough not to lock himself into anything—especially where a beautiful woman was concerned.

"This won't get in the way of anything we have going on with our business arrangement," he assured her. He'd honed the skill of separating business and personal long ago. "Don't deny what you want when there's nobody here but us."

She shifted against him and then there were two soft thuds to the stone floor. Her shoes were off... now for the rest of her clothes. Antonio waited a beat to see what she'd do next and he didn't have to wait long. She wrapped her legs around his waist and scooted farther to the edge of the desk, securing him perfectly between her thighs.

"I'm not going to deny either one of us." Her hands slid over his forearms and up over his chest, finally landing on the buttons of his shirt. "But since we're leaving all of the outside world out of this room, I'm done talking."

"Sí, señorita." Who knew beneath this professional, conservative persona a sexy vixen was hidden? Aside from her actions, her demands were just as telling as to exactly what she wanted. Why was everything about Elise so attractive and magnetic? He couldn't figure out how she could pull him in from so many angles, from her brilliant mind to her body to her work ethic and family loyalty. He shouldn't let these overwhelming urges overtake his common sense, but there was no going back now. He was too far in and he couldn't just ignore a woman in need...right?

As Elise toyed with the buttons on his shirt, Antonio eased his hands to her waist and slid up beneath the hem of her top. The instant he came in contact with that soft, velvety skin, Antonio knew this woman was going to be his undoing. He'd been in town less than three days and already had broken the promise to himself, and even though she had said this would only be a one-time thing, he wasn't about to lie to either of them and pretend that was an accurate statement.

He wanted her now and he knew he'd want her again. Turning off this need simply wasn't an option, nor did he want it to be.

Her hands frantically moved to rid him of his clothes and what started as sultry and passionate had quickly turned frantic and desperate...or perhaps the desperation was on his part because he was just as eager to get all of these barriers out of their way.

Antonio worked at the button and zipper of her pants and helped as she shifted side to side to ease the garments down below her hips. His shirt fell to the floor, he yanked her pants off and gave them a toss, and they both went to work on his jeans, but not before he reached into his wallet and pulled out protection.

In a matter of moments they were bare, and he was sheathed and ready, but he'd never cursed darkness more. What had been sexy and mysterious just moments ago, now only left him feeling robbed of the full Elise Hawthorne experience.

Oh, he might not be looking for more than a physical distraction, but that didn't mean he wanted to lose out on seeing this fascinating woman up close and completely bare.

Elise's hands flattened on his chest as her calves slid over his hips and she used the heels of her feet to dig into the backs of his thighs. Her silent demand was sexier than anything she'd said so far and Antonio wasted no time stepping into her.

Her hands traveled down his torso, then back up and over his shoulders, moving around to the back of his neck. She threaded her fingers through his hair and pulled him even closer.

He'd dated women all over the world, he'd bedded quite a few of them as well, but he'd never been with a woman who could pull off being subtle and dominating all wrapped into one alluring package.

And Antonio couldn't get enough of her.

As he eased in closer, he gripped her hips to make sure their bodies were lined up perfectly. She grazed her lips over his, almost as if trying to find her own way and how exactly she wanted to go into this. Maybe there was a slight hesitation because she was getting back into her mind, he didn't know. All he knew was that he wasn't going to let any outside forces into this room or into this moment.

Antonio opened his lips over hers, just as he joined their bodies. And then he stilled. He shouldn't have that immediate sensation of everything being so...perfect. Yet, there it was and now he had to get out of his own head space and into the moment because emotions or feelings or anything else were totally unwelcome.

All he wanted was to feel and let go, and let Elise do whatever she wanted.

Elise had just started having a panic of wondering if this was the biggest mistake she was getting ready to make, but then Antonio took over and she didn't give a damn if this moment, this night, was a mistake or not. He felt too good, *this* felt too good. She never did anything just because she wanted to. Her whole life had been giving to everyone else, taking care of others, and putting her own social life on the back burner.

For tonight, she was taking and not caring about consequences.

Having Antonio join their bodies so perfectly, and then remain completely and utterly still, was driving her out of her mind. Elise jerked her hips against his and arched against his bare body. What she wouldn't give to see those hard muscles in the light, but she'd have to just use her imagination because feeling them would have to be enough.

After tonight there would be nothing else between them other than setting up a nice VIP account and growing both of their businesses.

That sounded so cold, but there was nothing chilly about what was happening here and she wasn't going to be sorry or have regrets. This moment, this man, was exactly what she needed to get her mind off her grievances and stress.

As Antonio pumped faster, his hands came between them to cup her breasts. Elise tore her mouth from his, crying out as she dropped her head back and let every euphoric sensation wash over her.

Yes, this was exactly what she'd been missing in her life.

Antonio whispered something in Spanish and she wished like hell she'd paid more attention in school, but most likely her junior year Spanish class didn't go over whatever Antonio was sharing here.

He could be talking about a grocery list for all she knew, but it took this intimacy to a whole new level. Any man she dated from now on had to know another language and whisper something during intimacy. She never knew how much of a turn-on this would be.

His entire body worked against hers, his hands seemed to be everywhere at once, and that talented mouth roamed along her jawline, down the column of her throat, and to the swell of her breasts.

The immense onslaught of sensations hit her all at once from so many directions. She couldn't hold back, couldn't deny the euphoric combustion as she let go and let her body soar.

Elise cried out, reaching to clutch on to Antonio's shoulders for support. He continued to murmur something she couldn't quite understand and she couldn't focus on anything while her body continued to tremble.

Just as her waves started to cease, Antonio jerked harder, faster, then stilled as he rested his head just against the side of her neck. His quick, warm pants covered her heated skin as he struggled to catch his breath during his own release.

Elise wrapped her arms around him, closed her eyes, and continued to relish in this moment, to try somehow to lock it all in and freeze this portion of time. As ridiculous as it sounded, she wasn't ready to see their intimacy come to an end. She'd needed this distraction from her own grief, from her set ways. She hadn't realized how breaking the rules could be fun, exhilarating even.

And even though they were trapped, Elise wouldn't change a thing. She knew they'd get out come morning at the latest, so she was going to embrace their time together because once they left this room, every other interaction they had would be strictly professional. She'd go back to exactly the way she was before, but with a little secret she would keep locked away.

Silence enveloped them once again and Antonio shifted back, breaking that warm bond they'd created and shared. Now it was over, and she already regretted telling him this night was a one-time-only thing.

Six

His back had certainly had better nights of sleep. Antonio wasn't in his twenties anymore and he was about to say goodbye to his thirties as well, which apparently meant more aches and pains than he was normally used to.

But resting while sitting up against a stone wall with a sexy woman lying on his lap had been about the only option in this small space. Besides, it wasn't like he would have gotten much sleep anyway. His mind was too worked up, spinning in all directions about the quick events that had led them up to this point.

Antonio had certainly taken lovers and one-night

stands before, but last night had been new for him. He never slept with someone he was in direct contact with regarding his family's business, and he never slept with someone when he'd been vulnerable, but he'd been getting that same vibe from Elise. She was in a grieving period, so maybe they just needed each other.

It was all of these questions and unknowns that didn't sit well with him. He didn't like these unwanted emotions that had kept him awake and staring into the darkness. What happened to the times when he could just have sex and move on? It was like fate was mocking him by leaving him trapped in this room. Any other time he would have been itching to get out, to put the one-night stand behind him. And for reasons he couldn't begin to comprehend, he had no idea why he was so content still being here with no idea of when he would get out.

In all the hours he'd had to contemplate what he and Elise shared or what he ultimately wanted to do about his family business, he'd come up with absolutely nothing. He had no answers and the last thing he needed was more complications in his life.

Ironically, he'd just voluntarily added one and she currently had her face buried in his lap, letting off tiny snores that shouldn't be adorable, but they were. She'd probably be mortified if he told her she snored, so like a gentleman, he would keep that nugget of information to himself.

The lights flickered once, then went back off, then flickered again, staying on this time.

And the evidence of their passionate night couldn't be more obvious. Their clothes were strewn about all over the tiny space as they lay entangled and still completely bare.

Elise pushed off his lap, sat up, and clearly didn't want to look at him or say anything. She shoved her hair from her face and came to her feet, glancing around, deciphering her items from his. She scrambled to gather her clothes, keeping her back to him the entire time. No words, no smile, absolutely no emotion from the woman who had just bared everything to him.

Okay, then. Apparently, she was sticking to that whole one-night thing and they were not even going to discuss it. He hadn't taken Elise as someone who would turn away from conflict or an uncomfortable situation, but at the same time she was also regimented and a rule follower. She clearly meant what she said.

Antonio pulled his own clothes on, wanting to say something, but not really knowing what because he didn't want to make her uncomfortable.

Shouldn't something be said, though? They couldn't just pretend nothing happened...could they?

Maybe she could, but he couldn't. Something had happened and he wanted it to happen again, but if he couldn't even get her to speak, he'd likely never get her right back where he wanted.

Why couldn't they have both? While he was in town they could have a nice fling, since they both enjoyed themselves, yet still maintain that working relationship and partnership. The idea was perfect, but he had a feeling she didn't want his opinion right now.

Damn it. He'd never been like this before. He never actually cared about post-coital feelings or wanting to have a chat. What the hell had happened last night? When had he transitioned from fast, frantic sex to wanting to discuss it? He almost didn't recognize himself.

Elise smoothed her hair over her shoulder and turned to face him. "The electricity must have been restored."

"Then let's go before we get trapped again," he joked, though he wouldn't mind another night with her. Maybe this time in a more comfortable area with the moonlight on her skin so he could explore every inch and treat her the way a woman should be treated in bed.

Elise smiled, but her eyes darted away and he wondered if perhaps his joke came out completely wrong, like maybe he regretted what they'd shared. He had zero regrets. If he had to get trapped with anyone doing anything, this was the way to go about it.

After getting out into the hallway and then punching the code at the keypad at the end, Elise gestured for him to exit ahead of her. He started to pass by, but then turned to face her.

"I wouldn't change last night for anything."

Her eyes darted up to his, wide and full of shock.

"I didn't want you to leave this place with any negative thoughts or worries," he added.

Then, because he couldn't help himself and she'd still not said a word, he slid his lips over hers. They'd agreed that anything that happened down here stayed here, right? Well, they hadn't gone back upstairs yet and he wanted one last taste.

He swallowed her gasp, took a step into her, and backed her gently against the doorway. He pressed his hands on either side of her head, not the slightest bit ready to end this moment. There was something addicting about her and he had no clue what it was that kept pulling him in. Shouldn't their night together have already gotten her out of his system?

Unfortunately, the memorable experience did quite the opposite. He wanted more, so much more than those few hours had offered.

"Oh my word!"

Antonio pulled his lips from Elise at the shrill exclamation. He glanced over his shoulder to see Delilah, who looked both shocked and pissed.

Mierda.

Apparently, what happened wouldn't just be staying between Elise and him now.

"What the hell is going on?" Delilah demanded.

Elise pushed against Antonio's chest and took a step away from him and toward her sister. "Just a kiss."

Just a kiss? What?

Antonio nearly laughed, but he didn't say a word. However she wanted to handle this with her family was none of his concern. He had his own family issues to sort out and sex couldn't complicate his future. Hell, this had just been one night, he had no commitments or ties to her...other than that invisible pull he still couldn't quite figure out.

"A kiss?" Delilah huffed. "Is that why your shirt is on inside out?"

Elise gasped and glanced down, but Delilah let out a very unladylike growl.

"It's not inside out, but that reaction tells me more went on down here." Her eyes darted to Antonio, then back to Elise. "I don't even know what to say, but I'll be up getting things ready because Katie called in sick and someone has to head up the first tour of the morning. Maybe you should do the walk of shame back to your office and clean up."

Antonio inwardly cringed at the harsh tone as Delilah turned and left them alone. He glanced to Elise, but couldn't read her emotions. Gone was the passionate woman from the night before. Now she stood with her chin tipped in defiance, her arms crossed, and her shoulders back. A niggle of guilt curled through him, knowing he was the one to drive this uncomfortable wedge between the sisters, and no doubt Delilah would tell Sara, as well.

Family meant everything to him and he knew enough about Elise to know she felt the same. In many ways they were cut from the same cloth, but there was nothing he could do to change what had happened.

"I take full responsibility for all of this," he told Elise. "I can talk to her if that would make things better."

Elise turned to face him and shook her head. "No. We both are to blame and I need to take care of this. As far as work..."

She sighed and shoved her hair away from her face, then readjusted her glasses. The frustration permeated from her and Antonio wanted to take her into his arms to console her. Which would not be smart and he was a fool for even having those thoughts. He needed to push aside their night just as she was doing and focus on everything else going on in his life.

"I'll head out," he told her. "Why don't I come by tomorrow and we'll do the tasting for the exclusive bottles. I know we were down for today, but if that won't mess up your schedule, I'd say your sisters would like to talk to you."

Elise nodded, but didn't offer anything else so Antonio took that as his cue to leave. He should be elated about this easy way of escape, but he couldn't shake that gnawing feeling that he'd damaged something within Elise. But she didn't need or want him to interfere with her family dynamics or try to soothe the hurt feelings. She had to do that on her own and he had to delete last night from his memory.

Unfortunately, that was all he could think about and he knew without a shadow of a doubt that as long as he remained in Benton Springs, he would continually want Elise and that one time had certainly not been enough.

Considering they had a full day of tours and were down one employee, that left Elise stewing in her office until Delilah could come talk to her. Hopefully, by the time that happened, her sister would have cooled off a little.

After a change of clothes and a retouch of makeup and hair in her office bathroom, Elise felt a little more like she was ready to tackle any argument. But she couldn't stop thinking about last night. There was no way to just flip that switch and pretend it never happened. Oh, she'd put on what she hoped was a convincing front for Antonio earlier. She'd told him one night and that was what she had to hold to so she'd put that wall between them.

From here on out, they had to be professionals... no matter how her body still hummed and craved his touch. She'd just been without intimacy for so long, now her emotions had opened back up and she thought she had to have more. There was no way round two was even possible.

How had she gotten into this predicament? Could she be more cliché? A stormy night, a power outage, a sexy stranger. She'd allowed herself to be caught in that web of desire. Perhaps that was because she'd put herself directly in the path of seduction.

In the back of her mind, she knew what she'd been doing when she invited Antonio back into the distillery after hours. Granted, she couldn't have predicted the power outage, but she'd wanted to be alone with him; she'd wanted to continue feeling that sexual tension that she hadn't experienced in so long.

Elise pulled up her emails, determined to regain focus and get to work like she was supposed to do. They had a gala coming up, they had customers flying in from all over the country and potential customers from around the globe. This monumental night had zero room for error and all eyes would be on the three women who were going up against corporations and a male-dominated world.

Before she could open her first message, her office door slammed shut.

"Tell me this isn't true."

Elise glanced up to see Sara striding across the room, her long bangs flying around her face, as she held her cell up with her text screen open. Elise didn't have to read what the text was or who it was from to know what had happened.

"The kiss?" Elise asked. "It's true."

"Kiss?" Sara laughed. "This is me you're talking to. I'm not stupid and I've seen Antonio for myself. Nobody could blame you for what went on in that cellar. I want details, by the way. But I promised Delilah I would do damage control."

"There's no damage to control," Elise assured her. "Delilah came in at the wrong time and is blowing all of this up into nothing. Antonio and I are both professionals."

"Who just so happened to spend a dark night together in the basement of a castle. It's so romantic and I'm jealous."

Elise rolled her eyes and leaned back in her chair. "Not everything is a romance novel."

Sara gasped. "Why shouldn't it be? This is the greatest thing that's ever happened to you."

Elise couldn't really disagree with that, considering she hadn't been on an actual date in over a year and hadn't had sex in longer than that. Of all the sisters to have a heated one-night stand, Elise would be the last one for that position. But she wasn't sorry it happened. She was, however, sorry she got caught.

"Are you sure this won't mess up our working relationship with the Rodriguez family?" Sara asked, suddenly shifting back to work mode.

"I'm confident we will secure this account. In fact, Antonio is coming tomorrow for the tasting of the exclusive bottles we will make for them. So we need to get those sample batches ready and set up by one."

"Consider it done," Sara replied with a firm nod. Then she tipped her head and scrunched her nose. "Do you want to talk about last night?"

Elise pulled in a shaky breath. "Not really."

Sara offered a soft smile. "Well, my imagination is pretty good and I only have one thing to say. Good for you."

Elise couldn't help but laugh. "I don't imagine this is what Dee had in mind when she sent you to see me."

"Probably not, but she knows me so surely she's aware that I handle things much differently than her. And Camden just had those divorce papers delivered, so the timing couldn't have been worse."

Elise pulled in a shaky breath and closed her eyes. No wonder Delilah had been so harsh earlier. Elise couldn't imagine the pain Dee and Camden were going through. They were two imperfect people who were absolutely perfect together. But they were human and had flaws. Apparently, they couldn't work them out and Elise absolutely hated that for them.

"I had no idea," Elise said, refocusing on Sara. "I'm sure she'll come talk to me once this morning rush is over. What else do you have going on today?"

"I'm actually meeting someone at Milly's place around noon because I finally ordered a dumpster."

Elise didn't say anything; she didn't know what to say. Going through their childhood home and trying to decide what was precious enough to keep or what could be deemed as trash was like continually reliving the fact Milly was gone.

How could someone's entire life just be placed into a container and thrown out? How could years and memories be simplified down to so little and the rest of the world just move on?

"We have to do this," Sara added in that soft, comforting tone of hers. "Putting everything off won't change the fact and she would want us to move on."

"Moving on seems like we're leaving her behind."

"She's always with us," Sara reminded her. "Someone as bold and vibrant as Milly would never be left behind."

"Do you want me to come with you?" Elise asked.

"No. I'm just going to make sure it's dropped off around back and then I'll come back here. I don't plan on going through anything today. Maybe we can all go in this weekend and spend a few hours."

"Doing this together might make things a little easier," Elise agreed. "I'll bring the gin."

Sara laughed. "I'll get the tonic and lime."

"If Dee is speaking to me then, I'll have her bring some snacks."

Sara waved her hand. "You know how she is and she'll need you, especially today. Let her cool off. She'll come around."

Most likely, but Elise had never been one to put herself in drama or conflict. She absolutely hated confrontation, so this waiting game and the unknown of how Delilah would be was weighing heavy on Elise's mind.

"I need to get some work done before I head out," Sara stated. "If you ever want to talk about last night, let me know. And I don't just mean details. This is so out of character for you. If you just need someone to listen, I'm here."

Elise smiled and nodded before turning back to her computer. She wasn't sure she'd ever want to talk about that night with anybody. Discussing the events would only make her relive them over and over.

Then again, she'd be doing that anyway. There was no way she could go on with her life like she hadn't had the most intense sexual night ever. She almost felt like she needed to categorize everything that happened before Antonio and after Antonio. The man was that potent that she couldn't just pretend her life hadn't been altered forever.

And she still had to face him for work…like she hadn't spent a wild night with him and then woken up completely naked in his lap.

Seven

"What are your thoughts on Angel's Share?"

Antonio set his phone on speaker and placed it on the side table next to his Adirondack chair on the deck. He'd wanted to call and check in with his parents and, in true Carlos Rodriguez fashion, his father got right down to business.

But what Antonio thought of Angel's Share today was a bit different than what he'd thought yesterday. Now all Antonio could think of was Elise and all of that pent-up passion she'd unleashed on him. How intense she'd been, even though she tried so hard to shield her emotions…he'd felt them. When she'd initiated that first kiss, Antonio knew that had to have taken all of her courage to just go for what she wanted.

Which meant she'd truly desired him more than he'd first thought.

That in and of itself was one of the sexiest things about her. Aside from the fact she was brilliant and a master distiller, the woman knew what she wanted and went after it…in her personal and professional life.

"It's an impressive distillery," Antonio replied as he looked out over the rolling hills of Kentucky. "The samples I tried were great and just what I think we need to add to our restaurants. I'll be doing the exclusive tastings and will choose the best combination for us."

Most distillers would create a special batch for VIP clients or restaurateurs. Angel's Share was no different. To have an exclusive bourbon for Rodriguez establishments would be a win-win for both parties. Elise would get her label abroad and he would have something no one in Spain had gotten their hands on.

"And how is everything else going? I only traveled to Kentucky once many years ago. Beautiful part of the world."

"It is," Antonio agreed, not really in the mood for small talk with his father. "When I return home next month, I do have a few things I'd like to run by you."

There. He'd planted the seed for a talk. Although

Antonio still had no clue what that talk would entail exactly, he was hoping for some eye-opening experience while he was in the States. He was a damn good businessman, he just didn't know where he wanted to invest his time or his money quite yet.

"Sounds serious. Is everything okay?"

"Everything is fine," he assured his father. "Just looking ahead to the future."

"Well, that sounds promising. Your mother and I can't wait to turn over Rodriguez to the new generation. We're proud of you, *hijo*."

Damn it. He didn't want to feel guilty about pursuing his own plans, but he did. His parents had done absolutely everything for him and he was going to crush their dreams.

His father went on to tell him about some of the things that had happened since he left and how his mother was already booking trips to travel around the globe as soon as they handed over the reins. Antonio simply listened, because there wasn't much he could say and he couldn't get too excited about this transition because if he didn't have a solid plan, something tangible to cling to for his future, he would be stuck in a world he didn't love and didn't want.

He had too many passions, that was the problem. He loved to travel; he loved to meet new people and socialize, and he'd always been comfortable inserting himself into any situation. So staying locked down to one area, one business with many chains, seemed like a prison.

While he was damn proud of all his parents had accomplished, that wasn't his ultimate goal in life. For the past several years he'd done everything just as his parents wished. He didn't know another way without hurting them. Even though Paolo passed years ago, that was something none of them had recovered from. There was no recovery, there was only living a completely new chapter in life.

Grief had always been the driving force behind Antonio's actions. He was the only child left to make sure his parents had the happiness they deserved.

"Make sure to let me know how the exclusive tasting goes and what you decide on," his father said. "We trust your judgment."

"I'll call as soon as I've sealed a deal," he assured his father. "Talk to you then."

Antonio tapped the screen to hang up and stretched his legs out, crossing his ankles. He really had no plans today, though he should come up with something. Staying at his rental with just his thoughts regarding his home life and last night would only drive him mad.

Granted, last night hadn't been planned and today should have been his private tasting. But other events had unfolded and left him and Elise in a compromising position…literally.

He couldn't help but wonder how her day was

going and if there was too much of a rift between the sisters. Delilah seemed pretty upset and angry with Elise.

Antonio didn't know how his next visit would go, but perhaps taking a drive to see the picturesque area he'd never been before would clear his mind. Maybe he'd even find another restaurant that intrigued him. As someone who grew up in that business, he was always looking for new foods or atmosphere or anything that kept customers coming back. He might not want to do that line of work for life, but he still admired what his parents had established.

Was that to be his destiny? Should he just take over the life his parents wanted him to, especially now that they were opening pubs as their last big venture before they retired?

Antonio had always prided himself on being in control and making his own way in life. Even though he worked for his parents, he'd never been given a handout. His parents had always instilled a work ethic in him and he'd started at the bottom within the company. They'd wanted him to learn every position so he could fully understand staffing and be more relatable when he took over.

Antonio came to his feet and grabbed his cell from the accent table. He definitely needed to get out, get some fresh air and go for a drive. Maybe then he would have a clearer understanding and could regain focus of the reason he came to the US to begin with. His night with Elise was clouding his mind. When he should be planning his future, all he could think about was the sexy vixen who had seduced him in a mostly innocent, yet demanding way. Then again, how could he not be stuck replaying their night over and over?

"I never said Antonio and I did anything."

Delilah rolled her eyes and snorted. "You can't lie to me, Elise. I know what I saw and that was definitely a morning-after kiss."

Elise resisted the urge to pace her office, though there was plenty of room and she desperately needed to get some energy out of her system. She'd known Delilah would come and talk to her once she got a free minute, but there was nothing Elise could say at this point that would make her sister any less angry.

They all knew there was a different set of rules to live by, considering they were living in this man's world. They had to be careful of every action that could impact this business they'd taken years to build.

Though Elise knew the anger was well placed, all of Delilah's emotions likely stemmed from hurt. Delilah didn't want that divorce, but she was too damn stubborn to say otherwise.

"What were you thinking?" Delilah demanded, then held her hand out. "No, don't answer that. I've seen him, so I know exactly what you were thinking. But this isn't like you. This is something Sara would do."

Elise threw her arms out and sighed. "Fine. I'm human. Happy now?"

Delilah's pale pink lips pursed as her eyes narrowed. "Well, at least you're not lying to me anymore. But seriously. How is this going to affect our working relationship with that family?"

Elise crossed the room to stand in front of her sister, then calmly reached for her hands.

"There's nothing to worry about," Elise assured her. "Antonio and I are adults. We already said anything that happened last night was to stay a secret and had nothing to do with our partnership."

Delilah's worry lines between her brows only deepened. "Partnership aside, what on earth? I mean, seriously. You just met the man and the emails before he arrived do not count. Emotionally, this has to be eating at you."

Not in the way Delilah might think. The only thing that bothered Elise was how much she still desired Antonio. Having him once, okay, she couldn't really be to blame for her actions at her moment of weakness. But still having that need? Those unfamiliar emotions were certainly new for her.

All she could blame this on was the lack of social life and she was still in the grieving process since losing Milly. Vulnerable emotions had to be the reason for acting so out of character.

Fine. Those were all solid excuses, but she was a grown-ass woman who could make her own decisions and shouldn't have to justify or apologize.

"I'd rather just move on and put this behind all of us." Elise released her sister's hands and took a step back. "We have the VIP tasting scheduled for tomorrow. Antonio enjoyed all of the samples he tried yesterday. I really think he's going to have a difficult time narrowing down his decisions with our exclusive bottles. Now, do you want to discuss the papers you were delivered?"

Delilah held Elise's stare and ultimately shook her head. "Not particularly."

"Fine." Elise knew her sister would talk when she was good and ready. "Back to the tastings. Everything will be set up by noon. Antonio is coming at one and with the amount of new pubs his family is opening, I can't imagine he will leave without an astronomical partnership."

"Perhaps you can convince him to sign up for more than one batch," Delilah suggested. "Apparently—"

"You guys."

Elise and Delilah both jerked their attention toward the doorway where Sara stood, her face pale and eyes wide. She had a folder in her hand and she not only shut the door behind her, she also flicked the lock into place.

"What is it?" Elise demanded, crossing to Sara. "You're trembling."

Without a word, Sara thrust the folder against Elise's chest. "I don't know what to believe anymore. I just... I can't... Why all the secrets?"

"Okay, whatever it is, we will get through this." Delilah put her arm around Sara's shoulder. "Come have a seat and tell us what happened."

Elise shot a glance to Delilah, who shrugged, clearly just as confused and concerned. Sara usually wasn't dramatic, so whatever contents she'd uncovered in that folder had to be something rather serious.

"I found that in Milly's basement." Sara took a seat and placed her hands on her lap. "The guy for the dumpster was running late, so I just went downstairs to start sorting and looking. You know that old safe she always told us was empty? Well, I went to move it and heard something inside. It took me forever, and ultimately a hammer, but I got it open and that was in there."

Elise rested a hip against her desk while Delilah took a seat in the chair next to Sara. All eyes locked on the closed mystery folder.

"What is this that you keep referring to?"

Sara pulled in a shaky breath. "Our adoption papers, birth certificates, and look at that photograph of us as babies with a woman who looks like Milly, but that's not her."

Delilah and Elise studied all of the contents, but focused on the yellow-edged photo. Who was the mystery woman?

"Look at all the countless messages and receipts from a private investigator all trying to locate us," Sara added.

"An investigator?" Dee asked. "Why did Milly have an investigator? And what do you mean by *us*?"

"Because she was looking for you guys and me," Sara explained. "Before she ever adopted us, she was looking specifically for three girls."

Elise shook her head, having no idea what her sister was talking about. "How is that possible? She didn't even know who we were until she adopted us."

With a quick flip of the folder that she took back from Elise, Sara started sorting through the stack of papers. "That's what she wanted everyone to think. But from all of the papers and documents in here, Milly Hawthorne is our biological aunt."

"What?" Delilah gasped. "That's not possible."

Elise stared at the papers, as if she could see everything all at once and figure out what Sara was trying to say.

"Our birth mother was Milly's sister." Sara pulled out several papers and held them up. "We all have different fathers, but we share the same mother... and I believe that's the woman in the photograph with us."

Elise really wished she'd taken an actual seat before that bomb was dropped into her life. Real sisters? How was that even possible when they were all so different physically? There had to be some mistake, but whatever Sara had read, she firmly believed it to be the truth.

Her focus darted back to the picture as she studied the woman she'd never known. Could this be her mother? Milly's sister? There was so much to process here.

"Let me see," Delilah demanded as she took the papers. "None of this makes sense. If we have the same birth mother, where is she and why did Milly have to come looking for us?"

Sara closed her eyes and sighed before she refocused on the contents of the folder. She shuffled through once more and pulled up another paper.

"This is our biological mother's death certificate."

Death? They'd just supposedly found out who their birth mother was, one Elise still couldn't believe they shared, and now they discover she's no longer living? Were their lives condensed to this one folder? How could the history and all the answers they wanted be compiled into just these papers?

Elise's mind was spinning in way too many directions for her to keep up with. She wanted answers, but she really didn't know all the questions she wanted to ask.

"Her name was Carla Akers," Delilah stated as

she stared at the paper. "We have an actual name to put to the woman we don't even remember."

"She died in prison," Sara murmured. "When she went to prison, that's when Milly started looking for us. We were in different foster homes because of the overload of caregivers. It's all in there. Everything."

Elise rounded her desk and wheeled her chair back to the other side to take a seat next to Sara. Papers, documents, photographs, and photocopies were passed around the trio. Shock settled in quickly, and Elise was only left with more questions than she had answers for.

And there was no one left to ask.

"Am I reading this right?" Elise asked as she glanced to her sisters. "Our mom and Milly were estranged sisters. That's why she hired the investigator to find us after Mom ended up going away."

What kind of life had she led that ultimately took her down a path of destruction? How could she and Milly have been so different? Moreover, how could their birth mother be so totally opposite from each of her girls?

None of them had ever dabbled in drugs, they'd never been arrested. The closest run-in any of them had with the law was when Delilah got a speeding ticket after she'd left her purse at a restaurant and was hauling ass back to get it.

But now, reading all of these damning truths they couldn't deny, it just seemed like too much. There were too many raw emotions, especially coming on the coattails of Milly's death. She wouldn't have all of these papers if this wasn't true. But why hadn't she told them any of this?

"I just don't understand all the whys," Sara whispered, tears clearly clogging her throat. "Why had she never told us we were actually related? I mean, maybe she was protecting us from our mother's harsh life, but to know we are actually sisters..."

Elise thought back to all the years they'd spent with Milly and how she had truly loved and cared for them as her own. How she'd raised them as true sisters and they'd really never known any different since they'd come to live with her when they'd been so little. Of course they didn't remember being anywhere else but Milly's house.

"I agree," Elise stated. "In her own way, she probably wanted to protect us from the truth about our birth mom. Do I wish she would have told us the truth? Yes. But at the same time, she had a sister who was an addict, according to the paperwork here and her prison record. Milly was doing the best she could with three kids. Milly didn't have to come looking for us and I think that shows the love from the start that she had."

There wasn't a doubt in Elise's mind that Milly had moved heaven and earth to find them. The woman had worked as a schoolteacher her entire life and then a yoga instructor for fun on the side.

No doubt hiring an investigator took up most if not all of her savings.

Another burst of hurt struck Elise right in the chest. She missed that woman more than she ever thought possible to miss anyone. Would that gnawing ache and black hole ever be filled again?

"So what do we do now?" Delilah asked, her eyes brimming with unshed tears. "Do we pretend like we never saw this or do we try to get more answers?"

"Like what?" Sara asked.

Delilah sank back into her chair and glanced to both sisters before replying, "Find our biological fathers."

Eight

Antonio took a seat at the raw-edge table in the VIP tasting room. There were five tumblers before him, all with the Angel's Share logo etched into the thick glass. When he'd arrived earlier, he was greeted by an employee he hadn't met yet and was escorted into this room. He assumed Elise would be the one joining him, but after the other night, perhaps another sister would be taking her place.

Regardless, he was only here for a job so it didn't matter who showed up.

Which was partially a lie he kept repeating to himself. He wanted to see Elise again. He wanted to know if that sexual pull was still there or if she'd gotten out of his system. The only way to get that answer would be to see her face-to-face.

An entire day had passed without hearing from her or seeing her, so feelings and emotions weren't near as strong as they'd been when he'd left that cellar yesterday morning. The problem? All he'd thought about was what had transpired in the dark behind closed doors. Any other time he'd be thrilled to have one night, no strings, no regrets. But this night had been different in every way imaginable.

He should be amped up to find the perfect batch of exclusive bourbon for his family's restaurants… but he couldn't deny the fact he was much more on edge to see Elise. Ever since they walked out of the cellar, he'd continually replayed their night. As much as he had enjoyed the allure and seductive tone of being in the dark with such a dynamic woman, he'd felt robbed that he hadn't been able to fully see her. When the lights had finally flickered on, she'd been in such a hurry to dress, he hadn't been able to take in much…but it had been enough of a glimpse to make him crave more.

Well, damn. That answered his question. He still wanted her and he hadn't even seen her yet today.

Now, what was he supposed to do? She'd stressed their night was only a one-time thing, but how could she just flick off her emotions like that? She'd turned to fire in his arms and there was no way in hell she could just be done. He refused to believe someone as bold as Elise could just ignore this chemistry.

The door behind him opened and closed and he knew without turning around that Elise was going to be the one joining him today. Her soft sigh and floral perfume suddenly surrounded him. And he wished like hell she wasn't in the forefront of his mind, but she'd been there for two days now.

He was in some serious trouble with this one.

"Sorry I'm a few minutes late," she told him as she breezed by. "We had a slight staffing problem, but that's nothing you want or need to hear about."

As she came to stand on the other side of the table, Antonio noticed two things right off the bat about her. One, she was obviously frazzled and upset, which he highly doubted had anything to do with employees. And two, she was just as stunning and sexy as he remembered. Maybe more so, now that he'd had her.

Was it those glasses she pushed up on her nose? Or perhaps it was the way she'd pulled her vibrant red hair over one shoulder and let the waves fall down. He had no idea what this magnetic pull was or how the force continued to happen, but he did know he was having a hell of a time fighting it.

"I'm actually a pretty good listener," he told her, offering a smile.

She reached into the glass cabinet behind her and started pulling out five different bottles, all with different colored labels with a variety of names and numbers on them. At any other time he'd be thrilled to have this opportunity, but his hormones and this woman were trumping common sense and business right now.

"Yes, well, you're not here to play my shrink or sounding board," she retorted as she carefully sat one bottle by each glass. "You're here to choose the perfect bourbon to be sold exclusively for Rodriguez restaurants."

"I can do both."

He reached forward and took her hand before he could stop himself. Her eyes darted to his in an instant…and there it was. That fire he'd wondered if she'd been able to extinguish obviously still burned below the surface. No doubt she was trying to compartmentalize everything, but in a short time he already could read her body language.

The flare of her lids, the swift intake of breath, that quick yet subtle way she pursed her lips. The woman had become much too easy for him to read in too short a time.

"We need to focus," she murmured, staring back at him.

"I'm focused." He slid his thumb back and forth over the pulse on her wrist, a pulse that had kicked up. "Don't act like you're not thinking about it."

"Thinking about it and acting on it are two totally different things." Her eyes darted down to where his dark hand circled her wrist. "We can't do anything but put that night behind us."

He released her, only because he didn't want to come across as a complete jerk, but she wasn't unaffected. She wanted more with just the same amount of ache and need that he had.

"And how do you do that, exactly?" he asked. "Turn off desires so easily?"

She eased her hand away and shifted her gaze back to his. "Nothing about me is turned off when it comes to you," she corrected. "But I have a job to do and so do you. So that's what we should be doing."

Elise picked up the first bottle and started explaining what went into this particular batch and how this would be different from the others. As she poured, he didn't miss the way her hand shook slightly. Maybe others wouldn't notice that, but he'd fine-tuned her actions and this was completely out of the ordinary.

Once she sat the bottle down, Antonio eased his chair back, came to his feet, and circled the table. Elise jerked back and turned to face him.

"What are you doing?" she asked, her eyes wide as she took a step back.

"We aren't going any further until you tell me what has you so upset."

She stared at him another moment, then blinked and tried to look away. "I don't know what you mean."

Unable to help himself, he reached up and framed her face. He wanted to see those eyes, he wanted to see her, and he wanted her to see him. Damn it. What was he doing? He should be taking drinks and making notes, then placing a hell of an order.

But he'd be a complete ass if he ignored the fact Elise was hurting. Something had jarred her and he didn't think it had anything to do with him. Sure, their night had been amazing, but she wasn't this rattled when he'd left.

"And you think because we shared a night that you can read me so well?" she asked. "We agreed that was it, remember?"

Antonio slid his thumb over her bottom lip. "I never agreed to any such thing, but that's a discussion for later. You're upset."

There went those pursed lips again, but only for a second. She closed her eyes and blew out a breath before looking back up at him.

"There's some family stuff I'm dealing with that is private," she admitted. "I'm a little off today, but that won't hinder our time. I'm sorry you even noticed and pulled you away from what you came here to do."

"Will you stop?" he demanded. "You don't have to be Miss Professional right now. I know you're human, too. I also know you better than your other customers, if I'm assuming correctly. I can listen if you need to talk or we can reschedule. I don't want to cause more stress."

She opened her mouth, closed it, then shook her head. Antonio dropped his hands, but didn't step back. There was no way any business or work should take priority over what was happening to her internally.

"This is what I need to be doing and this is where I'm in control." She offered him a small smile. "I'm sure someone like you can understand control."

As much as he wanted to press, he had no right to, and if she wanted to dive into business, then that was what they'd do. He'd address their personal time later...because he was definitely not done with that conversation.

Elise waited as Antonio surveyed all the samples he'd had. He made notes on the paper provided by her team so the customers could rate the spirits in various categories and get the best bottle for their needs.

But her mind was on that damn folder in her office. There was so much to do with the gala coming up, their regular accounts and new ones coming in, on top of the public visiting each day, plus cleaning up at Milly's house...now her sisters were contemplating tracking down their biological fathers.

All of this chaos made that one-night stand look like a vacation. She wouldn't mind another vacation

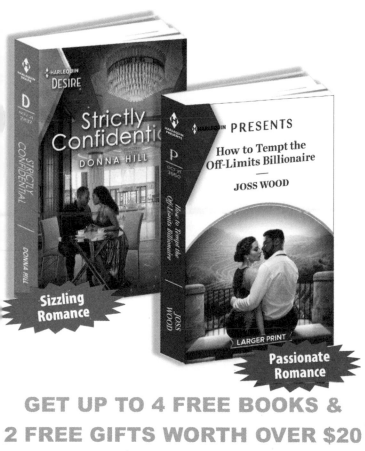

Treat Yourself with 2 Free Books!

Sizzling Romance

Passionate Romance

GET UP TO 4 FREE BOOKS & 2 FREE GIFTS WORTH OVER $20

See Inside For Details

Claim Them While You Can ⤳

Get ready to relax and indulge with your FREE BOOKS and more!

Claim up to FOUR NEW BOOKS & TWO MYSTERY GIFTS – absolutely FREE!

Dear Reader,

We both know life can be difficult at times. That's why it's important to treat yourself so you can relax and recharge once in a while.

And I'd like to help you do this by sending you this amazing offer of up to FOUR brand new full length FREE BOOKS that WE pay for.

This is everything I have ready to send to you right now:

Try **Harlequin® Desire** books featuring the worlds of the American elite with juicy plot twists, delicious sensuality and intriguing scandal.

Try **Harlequin Presents® Larger-Print** books featuring the glamorous lives of royals and billionaires in a world of exotic locations, where passion knows no bounds.

Or **TRY BOTH!**

All we ask in return is that you answer 4 simple questions on the attached Treat Yourself survey. You'll get **Two Free Books** and **Two Mystery Gifts** from each series you try, *altogether worth over $20!* Who could pass up a deal like that?

Sincerely,

Pam Powers

Harlequin Reader Service

Treat Yourself to Free Books and Free Gifts.

Answer 4 fun questions and get rewarded.

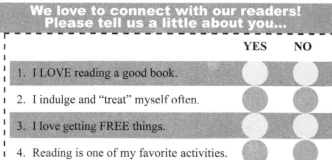

◄ DETACH AND MAIL CARD TODAY! ▼

	YES	NO
1. I LOVE reading a good book.	○	○
2. I indulge and "treat" myself often.	○	○
3. I love getting FREE things.	○	○
4. Reading is one of my favorite activities.	○	○

TREAT YOURSELF • Pick your 2 Free Books...

Yes! Please send me my Free Books from each series I select and Free Mystery Gifts. I understand that I am under no obligation to buy anything, as explained on the back of this card.

Which do you prefer?

❏ **Harlequin Desire®** 225/326 HDL GRAN
❏ **Harlequin Presents® Larger-Print** 176/376 HDL GRAN
❏ **Try Both** 225/326 & 176/376 HDL GRAY

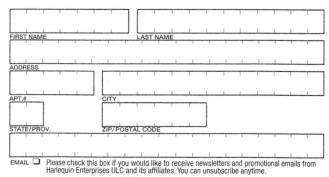

FIRST NAME   LAST NAME

ADDRESS

APT.#   CITY

STATE/PROV.   ZIP/POSTAL CODE

EMAIL ❏ Please check this box if you would like to receive newsletters and promotional emails from Harlequin Enterprises ULC and its affiliates. You can unsubscribe anytime.

HD/HP-520-TY22

to take her mind off all this, but she had too much going on to get sidetracked now.

Although if she was guessing correctly, she'd say Antonio was more than ready for another go-round. How the hell was she supposed to avoid temptation a second time?

"Well, what are you thinking?" she asked, mainly because the silence only made her start living in her own thoughts. "You seemed to really enjoy the gold and blue labels."

He nodded. "I really enjoyed all of them, but I want to narrow this down."

Elise crossed her arms and smiled. "You're used to just taking anything you want, I know. Must be tough to have to give something up."

His eyes met hers and that dark stare seemed even more arousing than before.

"I wouldn't know," he replied. "I've never given up anything that I've wanted."

One shiver after another raced through her. Of course he hadn't. She should have known that and she also should have known that anything she said could be construed as sexual. The awareness was too high and she knew this was not a level playing field. She didn't have experience like this with all the banter and the one-night stand. Someone like Antonio had skills she couldn't even imagine.

And she was falling way too easily into his web. The problem? She didn't necessarily want him to untangle her. Part of her enjoyed this thrilling stranger giving her memories to last a lifetime.

"Focus on the batches," she told him. No matter how much she would love to enter into a hot, temporary fling, she was still a professional in a man's world and she had to live by different standards. She didn't make the damn rules, but for now she had to live by them.

Angel's Share's reputation was everything to her and her sisters. This was all they had and she would not screw it up by letting a sexy Spaniard passing through get into her mind and jumble her priorities.

"Fine." He came to his feet and nodded. "We'll carry all of them and I'll make sure different batches are only available at various locations. Problem solved and everyone is happy."

Elise wanted to squeal with delight. They'd officially landed their first global account and not just a small one, either. She couldn't wait to tell Delilah and Sara. They all needed something good to focus on, especially now.

"All right, let's discuss us."

Antonio's bold statement pulled her attention back to the man who now leaned across the table, holding her steady with that dark, piercing gaze.

This is where things could get even trickier than they had been. The fine line she had to walk now would have to be done slowly or she'd fall off, and no matter which side she landed on, she'd get hurt.

"There is no us," she told him. "There was a night of intimacy when we were both vulnerable and now there is a working relationship. Thank you, by the way. Your contract will be drawn up by the end of the day and ready to sign and then you can travel across the country all you want, but know you got the best liquor right here in Benton Springs."

The muscle in his jaw clenched, his nostrils flared and she couldn't tell if he was aroused, frustrated, angry, or all of the above. Well, join the club because she was on her own emotional roller coaster.

"Tell me you haven't thought of that night every minute since we walked out," he countered. "Tell me you can just ignore the fact you still want me. Go ahead and try to lie to me, but you can't lie to yourself. I see it in your eyes, Elise. You're a passionate woman and you need an outlet."

Elise took in every word, and damn him for being so dead on with his assessment. How could he already know her so well? The fact that he could read her in such a short time should be a glaring red flag as to how many women he'd seduced and given this same speech to.

"Are you offering yourself up as my outlet?" she retorted.

Antonio shrugged. "If you want to use me, then so be it."

"How noble and self-sacrificing of you." Elise tucked her hair behind her ears and adjusted her glasses. She'd been wearing her hair down more since Antonio came into her life. "I'll worry about my passions and wants. I'm setting you free."

That wicked grin she'd seen before spread across his face, and a slow curl of arousal spiraled through her.

"Is that right?" Antonio eased back and stood straight up. "Your loss."

Yes, she was very well aware of that, but that was the choice she'd have to live with and she fully believed she was making the right one. She had to go with common sense over any wants or temporary needs.

"We can send the contract to you or you are welcome to wait around to sign," she told him, focusing solely on business now.

Something came over his face and that chiseled jawline seemed even more pronounced, his shoulders even more broad and squared, his defiant chin tipped as he stared back at her.

"Send it over," he told her. "I have some work I can be doing from home for the next few days."

"Consider it done," she assured him as she clasped her hands in front of her. Perhaps she did that for fear of reaching out to what she'd just shoved away.

Damn it. Why did she have to be a confused woman? Why did she have to put her career and family over her own selfish needs? Why couldn't she have it all? Who wrote these damn rules?

"This will be a very prosperous venture for the both of us," he told her.

Before she could comment or even think of what to say, Antonio offered her a nod and excused himself from the VIP tasting room. His long stride ate up the distance to the door and then he was gone, closing the door behind him. Elise stared at the closed door, knowing she'd made the best decision. If they'd met under different circumstances, maybe she could explore more.

But Antonio wasn't a *more* type of man. He was nothing but a fleeting distraction and she'd had her fun. Now she had to work and focus on this mess that had just blown up in her personal life…and forget that night with the Spaniard.

Nine

"Are you girls ready?" Delilah asked, shielding her face from the sun.

Elise stared up at the two-story old farmhouse in the middle of the Hawthorne property. She'd grown up here, she didn't remember any other home or anyone else who had ever cared for or loved her. But being back here with her sisters, knowing Milly wasn't on the other side of those doors, now more than ever Elise wanted her inside so she could ask all the questions this folder had produced.

All Elise could hope for was that they could find what they were looking for and then they'd have to deal with whatever truth they were left with.

"We won't find what we need out here." Sara sighed. "Let's head in and see what we can do."

Elise swallowed the lump in her throat as they headed toward the front door. Milly would have already put out her seasonal wreath and decorated her porch. There would be a plate of freshly baked cookies in the kitchen and each girl would be welcomed with a tight hug that would make them feel like they were home.

Death might have robbed them of the woman, but it couldn't rob them of the lifetime of memories they'd created together.

"Should we divide and conquer?" Elise asked.

Delilah turned her key into the lock and eased the door open. "That might be best. I'm afraid if we all stay in the same room, the only thing we'd get done is crying and reminiscing."

Sara laughed. "I'll cry anyway. But I really hope we can find some answers in here."

"I hope so, but if they weren't in that safe or that folder, I don't know where else they could be," Elise added. "This is all still so…overwhelming."

Elise followed her sisters inside and couldn't help but smile. The place still smelled like flowers. Milly always had fresh flowers from her gardens in various rooms. The grand staircase in the foyer led up to the bedrooms, so Elise started toward the steps.

"I'll go up," she offered. "Someone can take the basement and someone can take this floor. I'll be in

Milly's room. I know we need to clean out the whole house, but we're in agreement that we're looking for answers first, right?"

Both Delilah and Sara nodded.

"I'm in no hurry to sell this place," Sara stated.

"I'm not, either," Delilah agreed.

Elise bit the inside of her lip as emotions already threatened to overwhelm her. She had to power through. Mourning was a natural process, but there was so much to be done between going through and deciding what to keep or toss, and digging for more of the truth from their pasts.

"Then why are we selling?" Elise asked. "Nobody said we had to."

"Well, we all have our own places now," Delilah stated. "I mean, I guess I could stop renting that house and move back in here. I wasn't sure where to go once my divorce goes through."

Elise hoped the divorce didn't go through, but that was definitely a conversation for another time. There was too much other baggage to unpack today.

"Let's not make any major decisions just yet," Elise suggested. "We don't need the money from the sale, and one of us might just need this place. Let's hold on to it and just focus on finding out about our fathers."

"Is that what you want?" Delilah asked. "To find out who your father was?"

Elise had gone back and forth, wanting to know,

but also perfectly content with having Milly as everything she'd ever needed. But did her birth father even know her biological mother had been pregnant? Maybe he didn't know he had a child out in the world, and what if he'd been looking for her?

Or what if he hadn't cared? What if he was just as bad off as her mother, or had his own family by now and was settled in his ways? She wouldn't want to disrupt that.

"I honestly don't know what I want," Elise replied. "I'm just so confused lately."

"Are we talking the fact Milly was our aunt or the fact you're still hung up on Antonio?"

Elise jerked and blinked at her sister's accusation. Pulling in a deep breath, Elise gripped the banister on the staircase and eased down onto a step.

"All of it," she admitted.

"Oh no." Delilah leaned against the doorway that led into the living room and crossed her arms over her chest. "You cannot get attached to a one-night stand. I married mine and look how that has turned out."

"You and Camden are perfect together," Sara chimed in. "But we don't have time to argue about that right now."

Delilah opened her mouth, no doubt to argue, but Elise slid her own troubles in.

"I'm not used to flings, okay? And he seemed

caring, like he really worried how I was doing and the impact that night had on you guys with me."

"Men are simple creatures," Delilah told her. "They get what they want and then they move on. Don't read any more into it than that."

Sara rolled her eyes and came to sit beside Elise. "Don't listen to her. She's jaded. If you want to explore something with Antonio, go ahead. No one is stopping you. Do we think it's smart for the business? Probably not, but just think how romantic this could be."

Elise had no clue how her two sisters could be so polar opposite in their take on relationships. In all reality, she could see both of their points of view, which was why she was having such a difficult time figuring out where her head should be.

There was no good answer to be had right now and they each had other things they needed to be doing.

She came to her feet and turned to head upstairs. "I'll be in Milly's room. Let me know if you guys find anything."

The last thing she wanted was to get into a bickering feud regarding Delilah's upcoming divorce or to rehash her night with Antonio. She'd pushed him away from her personal life and neatly compartmentalized him in the professional pocket right where he should be...and where he would stay.

That didn't mean she couldn't keep reminiscing, though. She had all of those memories to last her a lifetime and one day she might actually find someone who loves her and wants to settle down... but would he make her feel so passionate? Would he make her feel so reckless and out of control she didn't care to vulnerably expose herself?

Honestly, she was so married to her career and that distillery, she couldn't imagine a man putting up with being second in her life. So Antonio was pushed aside just like she thought he should be.

Unfortunately, she still wanted him. He'd been right when he said he couldn't just turn off those emotions. She couldn't, either. But apparently, she was a damn good liar.

She didn't much worry for him, though. Antonio would move on to another town, another woman. That was his nature and he likely would forget her as soon as he found his next conquest.

Elise should be thankful her one-night stand was with someone not from around here. Once Antonio was gone for good, the temptation would remove itself and she wouldn't have such a hard time.

She sank down on the edge of Milly's bed and stared around the room. Milly was from the generation who saved everything, so each room would take so much time. Which was fine. At least Elise had something to do with her evenings instead of wonder what Antonio was doing...or whom he was doing it with.

Elise could only do so much and she had to focus on the house and finding answers. At least she could control that, somewhat. Keeping her mind on her sisters and their even deeper bond now was what Elise needed to focus on.

She started working with the narrow closet and the clothes. Each piece held a special memory, not to mention Milly's signature floral perfume. The boxes on the top shelf held old photographs, and before long Elise found herself sitting in the middle of the floor surrounded by pictures of birthdays and Christmases past. As she held a photo in one hand and one of Milly's favorite shirts in the other, Elise let out all of her emotions she'd been bottling up. The loss was too much for her to carry any longer, so she left everything right here where she sat. All of her anger, her emptiness, her sadness, her pain... all of it came out.

Finally.

Now, if she could only rid herself of those emotions for Antonio Rodriguez.

"You look as spent as I feel."

Elise looked up from her pile of photographs. Delilah stood in the doorway, her arms crossed, her eyes red-rimmed.

"This is much more difficult than I thought it would be," Elise admitted. "I'm not sure how far I got. Maybe this first day was just meant for an emotional cleanse."

"If that's the case, I'm pretty cleansed," her sister stated, stepping into the room.

Delilah carefully tiptoed around the memorabilia spread all over the rug and eased down to sit on her knees. Sara popped into the doorway right then as well and had a tissue up to her nose.

"Is this the pity party?" she asked. "Room for one more?"

"Come on in," Elise welcomed. "Move things out of the way for a seat if you'd like. I pretty much made a mess in here as I took a long, painful stroll down memory lane."

Sara circled the bed and ended up climbing on top of it just behind where Elise rested her back.

"This is like when we'd all pile in here when it would storm," Delilah laughed. "Milly always said she needed a bigger bed if we kept growing, but then we grew out of being scared."

"You know she loved every time we came in here." Sara wiped her eyes with a tissue. "She just didn't want to admit it because she was teaching us independence."

"There was nobody like her." Elise shifted her legs and scooped up a stack of photos. "There's so much love in all of these. It makes me think we should just leave things be and not go searching. We had a great life and I just… I don't know."

Sara started toying with Elise's hair. "I totally get it. I wondered the same thing. If Milly wanted us to know, then she would have told us. But she kept this truth from us for a reason and perhaps she was protecting us."

Delilah shook her head. "I want to know. I need to know. With all the upheaval in my life right now, I want some control and searching for my biological father is the only thing I can think of outside of work."

Elise glanced around to the mess she'd made and still had no clear picture of what she wanted to do. Each sister had to make her own choice as to what was right for her and they all likely wouldn't agree, but Elise knew one thing...they would all support each other no matter what.

"Are we done for the night?" she asked. "I'm exhausted and I'm not sure I can do this anymore today."

"Let's head out." Delilah came to her feet and reached her hand down to Elise. "If you all want to come back tomorrow, let me know. I'm fine taking a break, but I'm also fine doing this again."

Once on her feet, Elise shrugged. "I'll feel better once I get some rest. I will be here tomorrow for a few hours at least. Maybe if we do a little each day, we can find some answers or at least feel some sense of closure. Do either of you care if I take a few of these photos home?"

"Go for it," Delilah said. "I'm sure we'll all be taking some."

Once they all agreed to come back tomorrow afternoon, Elise took the precious photos and went to her car. The sun had long since set and she knew it was late. As tired as she was, she also knew that once she went home, she would be too wound up to sleep. There was simply too much rolling through her head. There were too many memories that had assaulted her over these past few hours. Her emotions were raw, like she'd just opened up her heart to all of the pain surrounding the loss.

From the overhead light in her car, Elise stared down at one of the photographs. This one was Milly with three little girls piled on her lap. Their smiles were all so wide, so happy. Elise didn't remember this day, but she'd seen this picture before. Milly had said this was the day the adoption had been finalized when the girls were toddlers. The day they truly became a family.

But they were already blood related well before then.

Elise sat the stack of images on the passenger seat and started up her car. She wasn't ready to go home and sit in the quiet with her thoughts and her worries. She needed something, needed someone.

So she pulled out of the drive and headed in the opposite direction of her house.

Ten

The soft knock at the front door had Antonio glancing up from his laptop. Who was stopping by so late? He only knew a few people and certainly hadn't told anyone where he was staying while in town.

He ignored it, thinking maybe just kids were playing pranks.

As he shifted his attention back to the spreadsheet he'd been drafting, the knock came again, a little louder this time.

Antonio pushed off the bar stool and moved around the kitchen island where he'd set up a makeshift office. He padded barefoot down the long hallway toward the front of the house and realized he only had on a pair of shorts and nothing else.

But the moment he glanced through the peephole, he realized he didn't need to be wearing anything more. The woman on the other side had already been all over him.

With a quick flick of the dead bolt, Antonio opened the door. He was about to blurt out some witty comment or something sexual to get their banter started, but he took one look at her and realized this wasn't the time.

Her eyes traveled over his body, then up to meet his gaze and that was when her eyes welled up with tears and she thrust herself into his arms. Antonio widened his stance to catch her as his arms came around her waist.

He had no clue what made her come here or what happened, but she had vulnerability written all over her. This was a bad, bad combo and he'd have to really pull up his willpower to resist her.

Still holding on tight, Antonio walked backward just enough to close the door. He reached behind her and slid the lock back into place. Elise buried her face in his neck and trembled against him. Whatever she'd gone through tonight had her seriously rattled.

"Are you hurt?" he asked.

"Just my heart," she whispered back.

Then she eased back and framed his face with her hands. She stared at him with unshed tears in her eyes and Antonio really wanted to harden himself against this woman. She'd made it clear their night was over and there would be no more. He didn't want to give in to her obvious, yet silent, request. He didn't want to be someone's regret in the morning.

"This is a bad idea," he told her. "Why don't you let me take you home?"

"If I wanted to go home, I'd be there," she murmured, her eyes dipping to his mouth. "But I need you. I need to forget reality for a little while. I'm not asking for anything else."

His body stirred to life and Antonio was trying to remember why this was a bad idea. She clearly knew what she was here for, she knew there was nothing else between them.

But she was vulnerable. Maybe too vulnerable to be making a rational decision.

"I know what I'm doing," she stated, as if she could read his thoughts. "Are you going to help me forget or not?"

Oh hell. He was fighting a losing battle. He knew it the moment he'd seen her standing on the other side of his door. She felt too damn good in his arms and she was on the verge of begging. Who was he to deny a distressed damsel?

Antonio lifted her into his arms. He had never been one for theatrics or romance, but he didn't even think about what he was doing. With one hand behind her back and the other behind her knees, he carried her to the bedroom.

This was nothing more than him helping her...at

least that was what he told himself. In all honesty, he was a selfish man who wanted everything she was offering. But she was hurting, that much was apparent. So he had to be attentive and nurturing. He had to let her take total control here.

Elise's fingers threaded through his hair and slid along his neck. Having her here was a total surprise, but he wasn't in the mood to ask questions. She'd come here for only one thing and he was more than ready to let her use his body.

As soon as he stepped into the room, he sat her on her feet at the foot of the bed. The light from the hallway flooded in and the full moon provided a soft glow through the double doors leading to the patio.

Antonio slid his fingertip beneath her chin and tipped her head up to look into her eyes. "You're sure?"

Elise flattened her hands on his chest and eased him back. Holding his gaze, she reached for the hem of her shirt and pulled it up and over her head. She tossed it aside without breaking her stare and then reached for the button on her jeans.

Antonio continued to watch as she rid herself of each and every article of clothing, and then stood before him completely bare. The light from the hall and the patio slashed across her body in various hues... he'd never seen a more stunning sight.

He'd known from feeling every inch of that skin just how gorgeous and curvy she was. But seeing her brought both of them to a whole new playing field. This wasn't like the other night. Oh, they might both be saying this was temporary, and it was, but the night they spent in the castle was spontaneous. Tonight...well, Elise had planned to come here with one goal in mind.

Still keeping her wide eyes locked on to his, she sank onto the bed and scooted until she was in the middle. She leaned back on her elbows and lifted her knees, silently inviting him to join her.

Damn it. Any other woman he would've been undressed and ready to go. But this woman... He wanted to see her, all of her. He wanted to take in each dip and curve.

"How long are you going to make me wait?" she asked.

Antonio remembered he'd vowed to give her the control and she clearly was more than ready for him. He quickly shed his shorts, went into the adjoining bath for protection, and came back in to stand beside the bed.

He looked down at her one last time before placing one knee on the comforter and crawling over her body to straddle her. With a knee on either side of her hips, Antonio placed one hand beside her head and used the fingertips of the other to trail down that smooth, creamy skin between her breasts.

"I can't stop looking at you," he admitted.

A slow smile spread across her face and he'd so

much rather that and the passion in her eyes than the vulnerable, hopeless feeling she'd appeared with when he'd first opened his door.

"I was robbed of the chance the other night and only had my imagination to go on since then."

Her brows quirked. "Been thinking about that, have you?"

He realized his mistake in admitting she'd been on his mind. How could he keep their fling isolated to one night, and now two, when she took up way too much real estate in his mind?

"Maybe I have," he whispered, his hand traveling down to her inner thigh. "I'd bet when you're in bed at night, you've been thinking, too."

He slid his fingertip just over her core and she arched her back, letting out a low moan. That was it. That was what he wanted from her. He wanted to make her forget whatever demon chased her here. He wanted her to only have him, have this, on her mind for the rest of the night.

Antonio was having a difficult time taking this slow, but she changed everything when she reached up, wrapped her arms around his neck and pulled his mouth to hers. She opened for him, grazing her tongue against his as she shifted beneath him. Before he knew it, he'd settled perfectly between her spread thighs and she'd locked her ankles behind his back.

"I need you," she panted against his lips. "Now."

He'd never found dominating women sexy before,

but Elise had a way that made him want to give up everything and just let her go. She had total control here and that was the biggest turn-on.

Antonio pushed into her, which elicited another cry from her as she reached up and gripped his shoulders. She tipped her hips and started working her sweet body against his. He kept the majority of his weight off her, using his hand to stay propped up. But he shifted and gripped the back of her thigh with his free hand, needing to be even closer, even deeper.

Elise's short nails bit into his skin, her head thrashed from side to side. He could watch her all night, but he wouldn't last...neither would she. Right now this was all about forgetting. Maybe in the morning they could explore even more.

Because she wasn't going anywhere tonight.

When she worked her hips even faster, Antonio eased down and kissed just below her ear, then along her jawline, and finally landed on her lips. She moaned into his mouth and Antonio wasn't sure how much longer he could hold back. When she panted like that, clutched onto him, jerked against him... she utterly consumed him and he still couldn't get enough.

Finally, her body stilled and she arched back even farther, breaking the kiss. Antonio couldn't tear his eyes away from the passionate woman beneath him. She'd shown up here needing him, but maybe it was he who needed her.

When she looked up at him with those expressive eyes and smiled, something flipped in his chest... which was ridiculous. That was just desire and want. Nothing more.

He jerked his hips as she whispered, urging him on. She pumped even harder against him until he completely shattered and let the climax consume him. He leaned down and rested his forehead against hers, trying to catch his breath, trying to figure out how to keep her here because he still wasn't done.

One time hadn't been enough. Two times hadn't been enough. At what point would he be willing and ready to let her go?

Elise lay in the crook of Antonio's arm, wondering how long she could stay wrapped in his embrace and in his bed. She'd come here looking for an escape, and she'd certainly found just that, but he'd been even more. There had been a gentleness to him that she hadn't expected. She'd assumed he'd open the door and she'd proposition him and they'd have frantic sex right in his entryway.

But no. He'd carried her to his bedroom like she was a prize he'd been waiting on.

She shouldn't let herself get giddy or read any more into this than what it was. All they had between them was just sex...and a working relationship. He wasn't going to fall madly in love with her and be by her side during all the difficult times. He didn't even live in this country, for pity's sake. So any form of emotional attachment was only asking for heartache.

As much as she wanted to remain right here, Elise couldn't let herself take more from Antonio. She'd gotten what she needed, a break from reality. She'd been so depleted after leaving Milly's she just had to have some sort of distraction and outlet. There was nothing more for her here.

Elise sat up and swung her legs over the side of the bed.

"Where are you going?"

Glancing over her shoulder, her heart flipped at the sight of Antonio. All of that dark skin glowing in the moonlight, his hair all messed from her fingers, and those heavy lids half shielding dark eyes as they stared up at her.

"Home."

Before she could come to her feet, his arm snaked around her waist and eased her back.

"Stay."

His lips grazed the small of her back, sending a shiver throughout her body. She closed her eyes, trying to hold on to the moment because all of this was fleeting and she had to lock in this intimate memory.

Oh, how she wanted to stay. But making that bold decision wasn't smart. If she stayed, they would be taking this from just physical to something more…at least she would. She made attachments, she'd never been one to have flings and she had a sinking feeling she was already getting too involved with this man.

"I should go," she countered.

Another kiss on her back, this one higher. Then another, and another. Finally, he reached her neck. Easing her hair aside and flipping it over one shoulder, he feathered his lips along that exposed skin.

"You should stay."

His hands came around from behind and captured her breasts. Elise dropped her head back against his shoulder and knew she was fighting a losing battle.

"I'm not done with you," he growled against her ear. "And we both know you don't want to go anywhere."

No, she didn't. And she wasn't.

Antonio slid one hand down her torso toward her core and Elise instinctively spread her thighs. The moment he touched her, she couldn't stop the cry of passion. He already knew her body so well and had spoiled her for anyone else.

"That's it," he murmured as he worked his hands all over her body. "Don't hold back."

As if she could. She had no clue how he managed to turn her on so fast and had her so achy in a matter of seconds. She started to think she was fighting a losing battle, but quickly realized she wasn't losing anything.

Elise let the euphoria take over, she let Antonio

have his way as he selflessly pleasured her. And when her body peaked, he murmured something in Spanish in her ear. She had no clue what he was saying, but that accent, that husky voice, was sexy as hell.

The moment she stopped trembling, Antonio shifted behind her and turned her in his arms. Elise came up to her knees, straddling his lap. She hovered over him and looped her arms around his neck.

"I guess I'll stay."

She smiled and eased her body down to join them. Antonio gripped her backside and worked his hands in a magnificent way that had her body already humming once again. His mouth found one nipple and Elise had to hold tight to his broad shoulders to remain in place. He totally consumed her and she wouldn't have it any other way.

She moved fast, harder, needing another release, and just as her body started climbing once again, Antonio released her breast and captured her mouth. His body tightened beneath hers as she let herself go. Strong hands covered her back, holding her even closer to that strong, hard chest.

The crest seemed to last longer this time, much more intense than ever before.

And when they both came down, Antonio cradled her in his arms, covered her with his blankets, and kissed her forehead before dozing off.

Elise lay there in the glow of the moonlight, wondering how she was ever supposed to let this man walk out of her life and go back to just a working relationship.

Eleven

The robust aroma of coffee pulled Antonio from his sleep. He blinked against the sunshine streaming in through the patio doors. He would have thought he dreamed of having Elise multiple times in this bed if not for his sore body and the rumpled sheets beside him.

She'd stayed. He didn't know why that had been so important to him, but he heard her bustling around in the kitchen and cursing beneath her breath. She shouldn't be so adorable, but he couldn't help but smile.

His mother would love her.

Antonio stilled. Where the hell had that thought

come from? He'd only met Elise in person days ago and was already thinking about his mother and her meeting? That was a big *hell no*. There was nothing more here than a fling and two people who needed to distance themselves from reality. That was all this ever could be.

Before he could get out of bed, Elise came back in holding two mugs of coffee.

"I assume you like it black?" she asked, then stopped in her tracks. "Or maybe not at all. I have no idea."

Ah, now a little bit of insecurity crept up. She wasn't acting so insecure last night when she showed up at his door. That was the bold, take-charge Elise. The woman who stood before him was having doubts and that was the last thing he wanted.

"Black is perfect," he told her, reaching for the mug.

She handed it over and he used his free hand to curl around her hip. She'd put on her T-shirt and underwear, but he could tell she hadn't bothered with a bra. Maybe she wasn't as conflicted as he'd thought.

"I'm surprised you didn't run when you woke up."

She offered a soft smile and shrugged. "I thought about it. I've never spent the night with a man I wasn't in a relationship with, so I wasn't sure what the protocol was. Especially considering our unique situation."

He sat his mug on the nightstand, took hers from

her and did the same, before urging her down to sit on the edge of the bed.

"There are no rules here, Elise. We both obviously have turmoil in our personal lives. There's nothing wrong with finding an outlet for escape."

Her green eyes seemed even more vibrant this morning than he'd seen before. Though they were still a little puffy from whatever had upset her before she arrived.

Do not get involved. Do. Not. Do. It.

"Want to tell me what had you showing up at my door so late?"

He couldn't help himself. He wanted to know what had happened to make her do a complete one-eighty from the last time he'd spoken with her. She'd been adamant they keep this relationship completely business. She wasn't even entertaining flirting...yet she'd spent the night in his bed.

Elise's eyes darted away and she pulled in a shaky breath. Antonio rested his hand on her bare thigh. Having this conversation while he was completely naked and she wasn't far from it was teetering extremely close to relationship status and deeper than he wanted to go.

Damn it, though. There was something about seeing her hurting that didn't sit well with him. He wanted to see the passionate, smiling woman who had all the confidence in the world...and she was still in there. He just had to pull that side back out.

"My sisters and I were at Milly's house yesterday," she finally stated, turning her attention back to him. "There's just so many memories left in that house."

"That has to be tough."

He couldn't imagine losing the foundation of his life. His parents had done everything to provide for him, they had made him the successful, determined man he was today. Which is why the guilt was so all-consuming and damn near crippling. He had to be honest, though. If nothing else, his parents had always demanded respect and honesty so there was no dodging this conversation.

Elise reached for her mug and took a sip of coffee before setting it back on the nightstand. He had no idea what to make of the fact she chose to turn to him when she was so upset. There had to be more than sex for her. She'd stated more than once that she didn't do flings, but they were sure as hell excelling at just that.

"How did Milly pass?" he asked.

"She had a stroke in her sleep." Elise slid her finger over his hand on her thigh and started drawing a pattern. "I should be glad she didn't know it was coming or wasn't in pain. But I'm selfish and I want her here. I have so many questions for her and after what we discovered…"

Antonio waited, but she stopped. He gave her thigh a gentle squeeze. "What did you find out?"

She pursed her lips and shook her head. "We decided not to tell anyone, but it's something that's changed all of us forever."

Disappointment hit him harder than it should have. There was no reason for him to care about her personal life. There was nothing he could do to help and he wasn't staying in town long enough to get involved.

Yet, he was a little upset she felt she couldn't confide in him. Who did she have besides her sisters? Who would she have turned to last night had he not been here? The idea of Elise turning to another man did not sit well with him. He didn't know why, there was no logical explanation, but he couldn't help how he felt.

Likely he was just too damn confused between his own life, which was up in the air, and the unexpected spin his world took when he met Elise. He'd told himself not to enter into any flings while here on work, but that was well before he'd been locked in a castle cellar with a vixen.

"My parents are expecting me to take over their family business in the next couple years."

He found himself opening up and he certainly hadn't planned to. But Elise was too easy to talk to and he wanted her to feel comfortable with him.

"That's actually the last thing I want," he admitted. "I love them, I love the empire they've built, but it's not the life I want to live."

Elise's eyes widened. "Oh wow. What do they say about that?"

Antonio shook his head and sighed. "Haven't told them yet. I was hoping to use this trip and some distance to figure out what I want to say and really where I want to go. I just know being married to a business and having to nurture it until I retire sounds like a bore."

She let out a soft sigh. "That's why I love being in business. I need a commitment and since I don't have any relationships, Angel's Share is all I have."

And that was just one way he'd found their differences. He didn't know why he was so restless, nothing in his past created that line of thinking. Quite the opposite, in fact. Family dynamics and solidarity had been ingrained into him since birth, even more so since the loss of his brother. But this was just not a legacy he wanted to carry on himself.

"When are you going to talk to your parents?" she asked.

"When I talked to my *padre* the other day, I mentioned enough to let him know we needed to talk about the future and the takeover. I don't want to blindside them."

Elise turned his hand over and laced their fingers together as she offered him the sweetest smile. And there went that flip in his chest again. He refused to believe his heart was getting involved. He'd never let that happen in his life, let alone with a woman he'd only known a few days.

"You don't want to disappoint them," she countered.

Antonio swallowed. "That, too."

"I can't imagine they'd be upset with whatever you decide. They love you and while I don't know them, I bet they want to see you happy."

He couldn't help but smile. "I don't doubt that's all they want, but if I don't take over, then who will? I'm all they have now since Paolo is gone."

"How did he die?" Her hand tightened slightly as she shifted a little closer to him.

"Paolo was four minutes older than me," he heard himself saying. "He was the best oldest brother, and I always reminded him he was older. We had the best childhood and did everything together, but he passed when we were thirteen from meningitis. Knowing my parents are looking to me as the next generation of all they've accomplished…it's overwhelming at times."

Damn it. He hated that he sounded like a jerk.

"I don't mean to be ungrateful," he went on. "There's nothing I wouldn't do for my mom and dad, but this wouldn't be fair to any of us if they handed the businesses over to someone who didn't want to be in that position. I keep hoping for a happy medium…which is why our inevitable conversation has to happen sooner rather than later."

"I think if you are completely honest with them, the three of you can find a solution," she offered. "Did you ever think they just assume they are doing you a favor? Maybe they think this is something you've been wanting. If you don't tell them your real feelings, they can't help you."

Antonio slid his other hand over their joined hands. "You're pretty damn smart. Have you ever thought of being a parent? Or do you even want a family?"

Well, hell. Why did he ask that? With every personal question, he dug himself deeper and deeper into her life. Pretty soon, he wasn't going to be able to see the top of this hole he'd dug for himself and there would be no way out.

The odd thing? He wasn't panicking about this. Not yet anyway. He enjoyed his time with Elise. There was something calming about her, something that seemed to temporarily fill a void he hadn't known he'd had.

Being here was good for him. When he left, he'd have all of these memories of their time together and he knew he'd met her, in this manner, for a good reason.

"I'd like a family someday," she told him with a shrug. "But I'm in no hurry. I'm terrified, actually. All I know is what I learned from Milly and now all of that turned out to be a lie."

What the hell had happened to her yesterday?

Whatever she'd uncovered was life changing and he wanted to know. He wanted to help her just like she'd helped him. Words from a virtual stranger seemed to go a long way in balming the wound.

"I'm a good listener," he offered. "I have nobody to tell your secrets to and sometimes an outsider's opinion goes a long way."

Elise pursed her lips and he could practically see that internal battle she waged with herself. She wanted to talk, to get this problem off her chest and seek some sort of relief, but he also knew enough about her to know she put her family above all else.

Just another way they were so much alike.

"Something like this could harm our business," she murmured. "I mean, maybe not, but other than promising my sisters, I also have to look out for Angel's Share."

Family and business. Of course. He couldn't be upset with that and he had to respect her decision. That didn't mean he liked it, though.

"First of all, I'd never turn any information on you or your business," he told her. "I respect your decision to keep this private, but you need to know that."

She nodded and removed her hand from his as she came to her feet. Before she could reach for her coffee mug, Antonio slid his hand up the hem of her shirt, instantly finding that curve of her backside. His body stirred to life and with no sheet or blanket to cover him, there was no hiding the effect she had on him.

"Where are you going?"

Her eyes traveled over his bare body, which sure as hell didn't help to curtail his desire.

"I'm supposed to meet my sisters this afternoon back at our old house," she told him.

He glanced at the clock on the nightstand and back to her. "Looks like you have plenty of time left."

He didn't want her to walk out of here, not yet. He needed more and had no idea when that ache of wanting *more* would cease. Regardless, he had a timeline here and there were other places in the States he was set to explore before heading back to Spain.

"Is it a good idea if I stay?" she asked.

Oh, he had her. He curled his other hand around her opposite hip and turned her body to face him. Staring up at her, he lifted that tee until it was around her neck, then she finished removing it, and flung the garment across the room. Antonio hooked his thumbs into her silky white panties and jerked them down. Elise scissored her legs to let them drop before she kicked them aside.

She climbed onto the bed and covered him completely.

"We didn't use protection the last time," he murmured against her ear.

"I'm on birth control and clean, but I guess it's too late for that conversation." She lifted her eyes to his. "Do we need something?"

"I've never gone without," he told her honestly. "I'm clean."

And there was that wide, sexy smile he'd come to…

No. He hadn't come to love it. He didn't *love.*

But he did want to see more of that happiness from her. He wanted to see all of her passion, all of her desire. And he wanted to be the one who gave her all of that.

As she joined their bodies and stared down at him with her heart in her eyes, Antonio knew he was in trouble…and he had no clue how the hell to make sure nobody got hurt when he left.

Twelve

"You have to wear blue," Sara told Delilah. "That's so your color."

Delilah stood in front of the floor-length mirror at the boutique dress shop and stared at her reflection. Then suddenly burst into tears.

Sara and Elise shot each other a quick glance before going to their sister.

"Don't wear blue," Sara corrected. "It's horrid. We'll find you something in black."

Delilah covered her face and sniffed. The sales associate came around the corner, but Elise smiled and waved her on.

"We're fine," she told her. "Maybe a glass of champagne?"

"Of course." The associate nodded and scurried away.

Surely this wasn't the first breakdown they'd had in the dressing area. They did cater to high-society women, after all. Queen was the store everyone went to when they wanted something different, something one-of-a-kind, and where they could be pampered while shopping.

With the posh pale pink velvet sofas, the crystal chandeliers, and mirrors all around, it was impossible not to fall in love with this place. Just the atmosphere made you feel beautiful and they wanted their customers so happy, that if they didn't have a dress you loved, they'd call in their custom seamstress to make the perfect dress happen for the client.

Elise had never gone that far. Anytime she'd come in, she fell in love with too many things and couldn't narrow her choices down. Although she'd never cried over anything, so something more than dress shopping was going on with her sister.

"I love the dress," Delilah stated with a sniff.

Elise patted her sister's back and honestly had no idea what had set her off right now. Maybe because of all of this going on with Milly, perhaps the divorce papers she'd been handed, or the fact they were each trying to find that perfect dress for their gala. This was about the only day they could carve out of their schedules to shop together. A sister's opinion was worth more than anything.

But right now Elise wasn't so concerned with finding the perfect piece for their bourbon reveal. All she cared about was the welfare of her two best friends because that was all she had left in this world.

"Blue is Camden's favorite color," Delilah admitted. "It was just instinct to grab this and try it on."

Sara glanced to Elise behind Dee's back. Elise just wanted to fix this for Dee and Camden, but there was nothing she could do.

"Then you should wear it," Elise offered. "You look gorgeous, for one thing. And for another, Camden will be at the gala. I mean, I'm not a marriage counselor, but maybe something as simple as a blue dress could get the two of you talking or reconnecting."

Delilah stared at her sisters in the mirror and patted her damp cheeks. "It's going to take more than a dress to repair this marriage and since he already sent me divorce papers I'm not even sure he wants to. We just have totally different ideas of marriage at this point."

She pulled in a deep breath and smoothed her hands down the front of the low-cut, floor-length dress. She turned from side to side on the large, round pedestal, and Elise and Sara took a step down to give her room.

"Honestly, it's really stunning on you," Sara stated. "You look hot."

Delilah laughed and turned to face them. "I actually do like this one. But maybe I should try more just to be sure. This was only my first one of the day."

She slipped into her dressing room just as a tray of champagne with cheese and crackers was delivered by the associate. Perfect timing. Champagne would surely help Dee not only get into the mood of trying on dresses, but it might also lift her spirits and help her forget just for a bit. That was what Elise wanted for this day. They'd all been bogged down with so much that they needed this relaxing, fun girl day away from work and life.

"What else can I get you ladies?" the associate asked.

Elise leaned in to whisper, "If you could spend more of your time on Delilah, that would be great. Sara and I can help each other. We just want Dee to feel extra special today."

The young, adorable associate nodded. "I can certainly do that. Just let me know if there's anything else I can get either of you, as well. I'm scheduled to cater to the three of you for as long as you need. You are my main customers today. I'll just go grab some of our accessories and shoes for your sister."

There were definitely perks to being a local celebrity. Or that was what the media had dubbed the sisters when they'd first opened. Anytime they went shopping or even out to dinner together, they were given the best treatment. Elise wasn't about to balk at all the people who were eager to help them. Queen did have appointments for their shopping experiences because they wanted each shopper to feel special and like they were looking through their own closet and not have to worry about bumping elbows with other women or vying for the same dress.

Once the associate had left the area, Elise turned to Sara and smiled. "So, which one are you trying on first?"

"That two-piece hot pink number is calling my name," she beamed. "It's sexy and romantic. It was made for me if I can get my top half shoved in there."

"Not all of us were blessed with such things," Delilah called from her dressing room.

Sara laughed. "They can be a blessing or a curse. I'll let you know which as soon as I try on the pink number."

Elise grabbed a glass of champagne and went into her own dressing room. As she stood there looking at the variety of dresses, she couldn't help but wonder what Antonio's favorite color was. That wasn't something they'd actually talked about. They seemed to have glossed over basics and gone straight to sex and heavier topics.

When she'd left his place two days ago, she'd so wanted to tell him her secrets. She wanted another opinion or just a listening ear. But she had to put her family, her business, first. Antonio wasn't staying, he wasn't a permanent part of her life so she'd had to take a mental step back.

He'd texted her yesterday, saying he was touring a vineyard about thirty miles away and then he'd sent a goofy selfie. She hadn't quite seen that playful side, but damn if she didn't immediately make that his contact profile picture.

Before she could think of it, she shot off a text.

Favorite color?

By the time she'd undressed, he'd sent his reply.

Your bare skin

Damn. He was good at this. But she could play this game. Something about Antonio made her bold, brazen, and a little more daring than she'd ever been before.

As luck would have it, she had a nude dress in here with a gold shimmer overlay. The deep V in the front dropped well below her breasts, and material would hug her every curve. Elise quickly threw the dress on and turned toward the mirror.

Wow. Even she had to admit she looked killer in this. But probably not the best dress for a professional gala for her distillery. Absolutely perfect for a selfie, though.

She cocked a hip, tilted her head so her red waves

fell over her shoulder, and put on her best heavy-lidded bedroom look. She snapped the pic and sent it before she could talk herself out of it.

Just trying on dresses for the gala. Thoughts?

Elise did a quick glance at the back of the dress, which was just as revealing as the front. She had no idea what she'd ever do with this one, but she'd never felt sexier.

She slipped out of it and put it back on the hanger just as her phone vibrated on the small table in the dressing area. She picked up her champagne and nearly choked on her drink when she read his message.

Buy it and I'll show you my thoughts

How could she turn down an invite like that?

"Oh my word," Sara squealed from the other side of the door. "The pink has won the battle, ladies."

Elise reached for the green off-the-shoulder dress with low, scooped back and fitted bodice. The satiny fabric looked like emeralds and she figured it would show off her eyes and hair.

"I'll be out in a second," Elise called. "Don't move."

She hung the nude-and-gold dress off to the side. She'd somehow have to sneak buying two dresses and not give her sisters any clue why she needed the other. That might be the most expensive piece of bedroom attire she'd ever invested in, but the fact that he wanted to see her again had her more than ready to splurge.

She quickly put on the green gown and stepped out of her room. Her eyes instantly took in Sara in the pink and Delilah, who now wore a short white cocktail dress with one full sleeve.

"Well, damn." Sara laughed. "We look amazing."

Elise went toward one of the free mirrors and stepped up onto the pedestal. She turned from side to side and really liked the feel of the gown; she also couldn't deny that green was definitely her color.

But it wasn't the nude and gold. Pretty much nothing would compare to that one because she was sure nothing else would elicit the same reaction from Antonio.

"I think the pink is it for me." Sara spun around and posed for her sisters to see. "Elise, you have to get that green. Tell me you love it."

"I definitely want this one for the gala."

"Delilah?" Sara asked, turning her attention from Elise.

Dee stared at herself in the mirror and wrinkled her nose. "I don't know. I like this, but I felt beautiful in the blue."

Elise rolled her eyes. "You're stunning in everything."

"Says the woman who is drop-dead gorgeous in that emerald green dress," Dee replied. "I guess I can't blame Antonio for seducing you. You are pretty gorgeous."

Elise chewed the inside of her cheek to keep from giving any indication that something was still going on with her one-night stand. She never hid things from her sisters, but she truly didn't think they'd like her and Antonio still carrying on the fling.

"Her face is red," Sara murmured a second before she clasped her hands together. "Something is going on. I knew it! Give us all the details."

Delilah jerked around. "Elise, are you serious?"

Elise darted her gaze between her sisters and there was no need in lying. They knew her better than anyone else and she had nothing to be sorry for. She was living her life, taking what she wanted that had nothing to do with family or work. This selfish decision was all about her personal life—one she'd put on hold for far too long.

"We have a mutual understanding," Elise explained.

"How is that going to work with the distillery partnership?" Dee asked, clearly skeptical.

"We have two separate relationships."

Sara stepped off her platform, still wearing that wide, giddy grin. "So you're admitting there's a personal relationship?"

"Having sex doesn't make two people in a relationship," Delilah retorted.

"Um...should I come back?"

Elise turned to see the associate with a soft grin and clearly wondering if she should come on in or turn and run.

"Oh, just girl talk," Sara replied. "But I will definitely take this dress if you'd like to help me with some shoes, size seven, and jewelry."

The associate nodded. "I know what would go perfectly with that. Give me just a minute."

Once they were alone again, Elise turned back to her sisters and shrugged.

"There's no relationship," she assured them. "We're just...enjoying each other."

"But you like him more than just physically." Sara tipped her head and narrowed her eyes. "I can see it written all over your face, so don't deny it."

"Please tell me you're not getting attached," Delilah pleaded. "Getting attached only leads to heartbreak and broken dreams. Trust me when I say all of this. The ending is always tragic."

Yet again, her sisters had totally different outlooks when it came to love.

Elise gasped. Love? Where the hell did that thought come from?

"What is it?" Sara asked. "What happened?"

"I've seen that look," Dee groaned. "Don't even say it. Don't think it, either."

Elise closed her eyes, as if she could reverse that thought. Clearly, she wasn't able to keep her facial expressions a secret, and if Antonio could read her like she thought he could, there was no way he could ever see that. The last thing she needed was for him to think she'd fallen for him.

And how was that even possible? After months of emailing, a few days of face-to-face, and some intense sex…that all couldn't lead to love. There was simply no way.

Yet, she felt something so deeply, something she'd never experienced with another man, and she had no clue what label to put on it—other than love.

"You cannot be in love with a man you barely know," Delilah stated.

"You think I don't know that?" Elise cried. "I mean, realistically, that doesn't make sense. But there's something so much more than the distillery and sex between us. I can't explain it."

Sara moved across the spacious dressing room area to the table with the champagne. She grabbed a flute and took a sip, her eyes holding on to Elise in the reflection of the mirror.

"That means it's real," Sara finally told them. "If you have all of those emotions and you can't describe it, then you're definitely in a relationship, Elise."

She thought back to their intimate conversation the other morning. He'd been so open with his past and his emotions. She hadn't expected that from him and she hadn't given anything in return. She'd so wanted to tell him what was going on with her family and she trusted him to keep her secret. Antonio knew the value of family and business, and she didn't think she was being naïve here.

"I don't know what to call it," Elise admitted.

"Trouble," Delilah answered.

Yeah. No doubt this could end up being trouble. What could come from a man who lived thousands of miles away and had commitments where he lived? Neither of them would up and move across the globe.

All of this was madness. Completely absurd. She should just tell him there would only be professional business from now on.

Her mind instantly went to that dress, that text, and she knew she wasn't done with Antonio Rodriguez.

As she met her sisters' worried stares, Elise realized Delilah was dead on. This was all trouble.

Thirteen

"So what are we doing about seeking out our fathers?" Sara asked.

Elise had barely gotten her cushioned chair scooted in at their favorite lunch hangout. Trinity had been open for only a few years, but already this upscale restaurant was thriving. They were another of Angel's Share's clients so the girls always tried to support them when possible.

Not to mention the atmosphere was absolutely adorable. Everything was set up in threes. The seating, the table groupings, the flowers on the tables, even the appetizers came out in threes.

"Right now I'm not ready to look." Elise reached

for her menu, though she always ordered the same thing. "Maybe in the future, but the more I think about it, the more I feel that Milly had a reason for keeping this from us and with her death still so recent, I'm just not ready to open that box."

"I agree with you," Delilah admitted. "But the selfish part of me wants to know."

"I'll support anything you guys decide to do," Elise added. "I just wanted you all to know where I stood here."

Sara tapped her fingers on her menu and sighed. "I can't help myself. I've given this a great deal of thought and I want to know. I understand what you're saying, Elise, but I just have to find out for my own peace of mind."

Elise reached for her sister's hand and smiled. "Then I will help you with whatever you need."

"Terrible timing," Dee added. "I've just got so much going on right now to even think of digging into my past. I can't get a grasp on my present and future."

"Have you talked to Camden since the papers were delivered?" Sara asked.

The waitress came just at that moment to take their orders and once they were alone again, Delilah shifted in her seat and rested her elbows up on the table.

"No," she answered. "I don't know what to say and I guess part of me was hoping he'd reach out, but I guess sending the papers was his only form of communication."

Elise hated hearing that; she truly hoped some miracle happened and Cam and Delilah could make up and get back to where they used to be. Delilah obviously hadn't signed the papers yet, so there was still hope.

"Let's not talk about that," Dee stated as she straightened up and shifted her attention to Elise. "I want to hear about what is and isn't going on with Antonio."

Great. That wasn't something she wanted to dive into and she'd thought they'd laid that topic to rest back at the dress shop. There was sex and a couple of conversations, then there was the business side. There really wasn't much else to tell...or at least nothing she wanted to share.

"You already know everything."

Sara cocked her head. "I doubt that."

"Well, everything you need to know," Elise amended.

"I'm worried about you," Delilah told her. "The last thing any of us needs is more hurt in our lives."

"I don't plan on getting hurt." Though she really wasn't quite certain that was in her control. "Just let me have a little fun."

"I think that's what we're most worried about," Sara added. "This is so unlike you that we're just afraid when Antonio leaves, you'll be crushed. You've fallen for him."

Maybe she had. So what? She was also a very logical person and she knew how all of this would play out. He would leave, she would stay, and they'd communicate via emails for business purposes only.

"No matter what my feelings are for him, I can handle it," she assured them. "Listen, we have something, I won't deny that. The physical is just one part of it. We've also had some pretty in-depth conversations and I just feel like he understands me."

"Did you tell him about what we found at Milly's?" Sara asked.

Elise shook her head. "I just told him we were dealing with some things that changed our lives and everything we thought to be the truth. But I didn't want to share too much since we agreed not to say anything for now."

"I wouldn't care if you told him." Sara reached for the pitcher of water on the table and poured three glasses. "I actually put out some feelers for an investigator. I hope that's okay."

"You want to find your biological father and that's the first step," Delilah told her. "And as far as Antonio, you do what you feel is right. I just don't want our business affected."

Elise would trust Antonio with anything and part of her did want his opinion, or maybe she just wanted an outside shoulder to lean on. Or maybe part of her just wanted that bond of theirs to go even deeper. She didn't know the exact answer, but she did know she couldn't wait to see him again.

"There's that look on her face again," Sara whispered.

Delilah nodded. "I see it."

"Oh stop." Elise rolled her eyes and reached for her water. "We're all trying to get through this crazy time together. Just let me have my fun."

Sara winked. "Oh, I'd say you're already having it. But I'm glad. I'm still holding out hope that this will be some dramatically happy ending and the two of you will fall in love."

Delilah opened her mouth, but Sara held up her hand. "No, don't say it. Just let me have my moment and let Elise enjoy this."

"While it lasts," Dee muttered under her breath.

Yeah, while it lasted. The clock was ticking and much too quickly, in her opinion. She wanted more time with Antonio, she wanted to get to know even more about his life and his family. She wanted him to not live so far away because there was no way a long-distance relationship would work with an ocean between them.

The man hadn't even mentioned anything about any type of relationship, so the fact that she was even thinking in that manner should be a glaring red flag that she was going to get hurt. But Elise took a chapter from Sara's romance book and chose to live in the moment and soak up all the happiness this time had to offer.

Antonio had left Twisted Vine Vineyard and returned to his rental, but he didn't like the emptiness or the silence that greeted him. Even though this was only his temporary home, having Elise here for a time had changed the dynamics of his entire stay.

What the hell would he do when it was time to move on from Benton Springs? He was due in Tennessee in just a couple of days, but he had promised he'd return for the Angel's Share ten-year bourbon reveal gala. His pilot was well compensated, so going back and forth would be no trouble. But at some point he would be leaving here for a final time and that idea didn't sit well with him. There was a knot of anxiety and confusion where Elise was concerned.

One thing was certain, though. He wanted to see her. He wanted more of her for as long as he was here and for as long as she'd allow.

Antonio unbuttoned the cuffs of his sleeves and rolled them up as he headed toward the bedroom. His eyes instantly landed on that bed, and an image of the two of them and all they'd shared instantly filled his mind. The time he'd spent with her in the cellar and here in this room had been the most memorable, erotic moments of his life. He couldn't ignore this ache of desire, not to mention whatever hell else was happening between them.

Antonio waited for about a half second before he pulled out his cell and texted her.

I need to see you. Are you coming here or should I come to you?

He sat his phone on the dresser and stripped from his dress shirt and pants as he headed toward the shower. This had been a long day and he just wanted to decompress and change his clothes. Then he'd be ready for Elise. He'd thought of her all damn day.

No, that wasn't true. He'd thought of her since the moment she left the other morning. Their conversation replayed over and over in his head. But even more than all their time conversing, he'd told her things he'd never told anyone. She'd truly listened to him, she'd offered advice, she'd even comforted him. None of that had to do with sex or their business arrangement. Elise was truly a phenomenal woman.

He wasn't looking for this…whatever *this* was. When he'd come to the States he'd been dead set on figuring out his own life, working on the pub side of his family's business, and keeping the entire trip professional.

Then Elise landed in his lap—quite literally— and he hadn't been able to concentrate on much else. Even during his touring and tastings earlier today at the vineyard, his mind had been elsewhere and that was the first time in his life he'd ever let a woman cloud his professional mind.

Part of him wondered how this happened in such a short time, but the other part of him knew there was something special about Elise and she just had that impact that was impossible to ignore.

After his shower, Antonio checked his cell and there was nothing. A surge of disappointment hit him. But he had no actual ties to her. They hadn't made any commitments to each other or even discussed meeting up again. He'd just assumed they would carry on this intimate relationship for as long as he was in town.

Maybe he should have specified exactly what he wanted from her. He'd thought from her sexy text earlier that they were on the same page. He'd been in the middle of his tastings when he'd checked his cell and nearly choked on his Cabernet. That damn dress made her body look like she'd just stepped from every fantasy he'd ever had. Antonio hadn't even thought it possible she could look even sexier than he'd seen her, but she sure as hell managed just that.

Right as he turned to his closet to get dressed, his cell rang. Gripping the towel around his hips with one hand, he picked up the cell, only to see his mother's name popping up.

He shouldn't be disappointed, but he'd thought

for a second the caller was Elise. Then a sliver of worry hit him as he answered.

"It's late there. Is everything okay?"

"Of course. I just couldn't sleep and wanted to talk to you."

"Of course." Antonio sank on the edge of his bed, still holding on to his towel. "What's on your mind?"

"That's what I wanted to ask you," she retorted. "Your father mentioned you wanted to talk to us when you returned home about the business. I've been thinking about that since he told me. I want to know what you're thinking because I have anxiety and can't wait for you to return."

He knew his mother was a worrier, what mother wasn't? But he didn't want to get into this on the phone and when it was nearing midnight back home.

"There's nothing to worry about," he assured her. "Just some life choices I've been thinking on and would like to run by you guys."

"I see," she murmured. "Are you having second thoughts about taking over or do you have bigger plans for what we already have?"

Antonio glanced up to the ceiling and pulled in a breath, trying to weigh his options and choose his words wisely.

"There's just a good bit to discuss in person," he replied. "I've had some eye-opening experiences here that have me thinking and my mind is in all different directions."

"What's her name?"

Antonio stilled. "Excuse me?"

"The woman you met," his mom replied. "What's her name?"

"How do you know there's a woman?"

His mother's soft laughter came through the line and he knew there was no lying here and no trying to talk his way around the answer.

"*Carino*, you're talking to me, so you might as well just say it. You have a different tone in your voice and something has changed about you."

She could tell that just by the five minutes they'd been chatting? What did that mean? What did she hear that could possibly make her think he'd changed so much?

Before he could answer, his doorbell rang. His stomach clenched because he knew exactly who would be on the other side. She was the only person who knew where he was and he hadn't exactly sought out other friendships.

Antonio gripped his towel and padded barefoot toward the front door. After a quick peek through the peephole, he nearly dropped his cell and the towel.

"*Hijo*, are you still there?"

He flicked the lock and opened the door to Elise... who stood before him wearing that damn dress that looked like she wore nothing but glitter.

"I'm here," he replied, his eyes locking on to Elise's.

She held her arms out wide and did a very slow spin right there on his front porch before turning back to face him and sauntering right on in like she owned the place.

"Mom, I'll call you tomorrow," he finally replied.

"With more details about this woman, I hope."

He couldn't tear his gaze or his attention away from those swaying hips as she made her way toward his bedroom.

"Yes, of course."

He hung up, not really comprehending what he'd just agreed to, but he didn't care. This woman was going to be the death of him, but he wouldn't want to go any other way.

Fourteen

Elise didn't know what had come over her, but there was some serious power in this dress. The way Antonio had answered the door, phone to his ear and gripping that minuscule towel that barely covered him, it had been all she could do to just walk in and not jerk that white terrycloth out of the way.

But she'd refrained. She wanted him to want her. She wanted him just as needy as she was. And from his text earlier, she had to assume he was exactly that. The moment she'd read his message, she'd thrown on the dress, brushed out her hair, and headed on over. She didn't want to think about it and she didn't want to give herself time to back out. If she'd put too much thought into this, she'd start feeling silly. Never once did she dress up for a man before. Lingerie wasn't practical and she had nobody to wear it for.

Antonio had loved this dress, so here she was, more than ready for him to peel her out of it and show her exactly how much he'd missed her touch.

She never would have had the confidence to do this with another man. How had he pulled her so far out of her comfort zone without her noticing?

"I'm glad that wasn't a video call with my mother."

Elise turned to see Antonio in the doorway of his bedroom, still clutching that towel in one hand and his cell in the other.

"That would have been an awkward moment," Elise agreed, propping her hands on the dip in her waist and cocking her hip. "Do you often answer the door wearing just a towel?"

In an instant, the towel fell to the floor. Antonio took a step into the room, put his phone on the dresser, and took another step toward her. Those dark eyes never wavered.

As her stomach quivered with anticipation and her heartbeat kicked up, Elise was so glad she'd opted to just go on gut instinct and show up here without replying to his message. This might be temporary, but she wanted to hold on to each moment she could. And maybe Sara was right, what if something came from this?

Elise didn't want to get her hopes up too high, but there was that flutter of excitement she couldn't help but cling to. She'd never had so many emotions, such a high, from one man before now, so ignoring any of this would only cheat herself out of something amazing.

"Do you often show up at a man's house wearing a dress that was made for sex?"

Elise shivered, but still managed what she hoped was a saucy smile. "You're my first."

He reached out, curling his fingers around her hips and hauling her against him. His mouth hovered just over hers.

"Right answer," he murmured against her lips.

His hands roamed up over her waist, to the curve of her breasts, and back down.

"How the hell do I get you out of this?" he asked.

Elise flattened her palms against his chest. "And here I thought you loved this dress?"

Antonio grazed his lips across her jawline and up toward her ear. "Oh, I love it. I've thought of little else since that picture, *pequena marta*."

Another shiver raced through her. "What does that mean?"

His eyes came back to hers as he framed her face between his strong hands. "Little minx."

And then his mouth covered hers completely, demanding her to open for him, demanding she make good on that unspoken promise that had gone right along with her sending that photo from the dressing room.

Elise gripped his bare shoulders, relishing in the fact that he had answered the door knowing she'd be there. They'd already fallen into sync with each other, especially where intimacy was concerned. But other things just didn't need to be said or discussed.

Antonio broke away from the kiss and spun her around. His hands were all over her back, her sides, then he cursed beneath his breath.

"Where's the damn zipper?" he growled.

Elise loved that she was the one who brought out that reckless side of him. Who knew she'd possessed such power or that she'd love being so spontaneous?

"There's no zipper." She flashed him a grin over her shoulder and smoothed her hair out of the way. "It pulls on and off."

"Misericordia."

She couldn't help but laugh at his whisper. "You speak more Spanish when you're turned on."

"Then it's amazing I have any English left in me right now," he countered.

Before she could reply, Antonio dropped to his knees and eased his hands beneath the hem of the dress. She'd thrown on a pair of heels only because the dress was so long and she hadn't wanted to trip…

that wouldn't have made the impression she was going for.

With his eyes locked on hers, he slid one shoe off, then the other. His hands slowly slid up her calves, then just behind her knees, to her thighs, and then he stopped. Elise nearly moaned, but she managed just barely to hold it back.

The dress bunched at her thighs as his fingers dug into her skin. She stared down at him, and those dark eyes held her completely captivated. She smoothed a hand over his jaw, then raked her thumb across his lower lip. His tongue darted out and dampened her skin.

"Spread your legs," he murmured.

Elise complied and he moved farther up with the material until it was bunched around her waist. Then he eased forward until his face was exactly where she ached the most. His warm breath fell upon her bare, heated skin and she was about one second away from begging.

When his mouth touched her, Elise had to grip his shoulders to remain upright. Too many sensations hit her all at once. The way he held her in place with that firm grip and his lips had Elise unable to control her emotions. Her body climbed so fast, so intensely, she cried out and it took everything in her not to fall over. Antonio made love to her with his mouth and she'd never in her life had this type of experience. Nothing prepared her for this man and the way she'd connected on so many levels with him.

Elise's body went weak and Antonio came to his feet, still holding on to her. He lifted her in his arms and turned, carrying her over to the bed. He sat her on the edge and finished peeling off her dress. He laid the dress over a chair in the corner of the room before coming back to her and staring down.

"You're quite exquisite when you come undone." He stroked her jawline and feathered down her neck, to the valley between her breasts. "But I'm not done with you."

A shiver raced through her entire body. She couldn't imagine feeling more than she did right now. How could he pull out so many different emotions and thrills?

"You already wore me out." She fell back onto the bed. "I'm not sure I'm ready for more."

Antonio placed his hands on the insides of her knees and eased them apart, then came to stand between. He continued to stare down at her with that dark gaze. Despite being depleted, her body still managed to start humming once again. All it took was a stare, a simple touch, and the man had her turning into a puddle.

"How about you just lie back and relax and I'll do the rest?" he suggested.

Elise smiled up at him. "You've done so much already."

"Good thing I have more to give."

He pulled her toward where he was standing at the edge of the bed. Still holding firmly onto the backs of her legs, he joined their bodies and never wavered that heavy-lidded stare. He moved against her, slowly, passionately. Elise wanted to close her eyes and savor the moment, but she couldn't. Breaking that silent bond would be doing both of them a disservice. There was something so much more going on here, but also something he likely wasn't ready to discuss.

Elise wasn't about to ruin the moment with words that stemmed from her euphoric state. At this point all she needed to do was enjoy the man, the moment, the night. That dress was the best splurge she'd ever made and she'd never look at it the same again.

When Antonio's hand slid between their bodies and touched her at exactly the right spot, Elise could no longer hold herself back. She lifted up to her elbows, now focusing on how beautifully their bodies moved together. With his dark skin in contrast with her creamy skin, they were different, yet so very much the same.

Elise let go of every thought and allowed her body to be all consumed with everything Antonio offered her. He was such a selfless lover and she couldn't imagine ever being with another man after this.

As she cried out her release, Antonio said something again in Spanish just as he held tight to her hips and let himself follow her over the edge. Elise slid her knees up his sides and propped her heels on the edge of the bed for just a bit more leverage…she couldn't get close enough.

Just as her body stopped trembling, Antonio eased down to lie on her. With their bodies still joined, Elise wrapped her arms and legs around him, wanting to keep him right here with her. She'd never wanted time to stand still more than right this minute.

What would happen when he ultimately left? This affair did have an expiration date and it was looming over their heads. Elise didn't want to think about that, she didn't want any negative thoughts to break into this perfect bubble they'd created.

With the way this whole thing started when they'd gotten stranded in the cellar, and then the chemistry…everything just seemed to explode so fast. Slowing down hadn't even been an option. Elise had hung on for the ride and enjoyed that thrilling exhilaration she experienced each time she was near Antonio. She'd never met anyone like him and she doubted she ever would again.

"I can hear your mind working," he murmured into her ear. "I must not have been thorough enough."

Elise laughed as she trailed her fingertips up and down his back. "You were thorough. My mind is always working."

Antonio pressed his hands on the bed on either

side of her head and pushed up slightly. With his hair all mussed, those dark eyes framed by inky lashes, and a slight sheen of sweat, she'd honestly never seen a sexier, more breathtaking sight.

"Do those thoughts include you staying here for the night?" he asked.

Every day, every moment, she seemed to get deeper and deeper, but she just couldn't say no to him. Well, she could, but why? She wanted this, she wanted him, even if all of this beautiful mess was temporary. They each had hectic lives, both personal and professional, but everything they'd created together was something only for them. Nobody could take this away and she fully intended to lock these memories in forever.

So of course she'd be staying the night. She still had more memories to make.

Fifteen

"Did you talk to your mother about what you want when you get home?"

Elise extended her feet in front of her on the chaise. It was well after midnight, but neither she nor Antonio were tired. She'd thrown on one of his white T-shirts and he'd pulled on a pair of gym shorts and they had moved out to the balcony off his bedroom. He relaxed in the chaise next to her and their glasses of wine sat on the table in between.

There was something even more intimate about this moment than all the sexual encounters they'd shared. Talking and diving deeper into each other's lives only pulled them further over the relationship line, though she wasn't about to bring up that uncomfortable topic.

"I didn't get a chance." He shot her a smirk and a wink. "Someone showed up at my door and distracted me."

"Oops." Elise lifted her hands in a mock shrug. "Bad timing on my part."

"Perfect timing," he countered. "It was late over there and that was not a conversation I want to have over the phone anyway. I'm grateful for everything they've done and instilled in me, but I have to live my life and not theirs. It's not fair to any of us."

"I don't know your parents, but I would think they'd be proud of you for wanting to live your own life."

Antonio turned back to look up at the starry sky. "I never thought of it that way, but maybe you're right."

Silence settled between them, but there was no discomfort. There was something so easy about talking with him and being with him that put her mind and her heart at ease. She found herself wanting to share more of herself, wanting him to understand her even more.

"We discovered that Milly wasn't just our adoptive mother," she heard herself saying before she could think twice. "She was our biological aunt. My birth mom's sister."

Antonio shifted in his seat and from the corner of

her eye, she noticed he'd sat straight up and turned to face her. Elise kept her gaze to the sky as she spoke, trying not to break down because this was the first time she'd said all of this out loud away from her sisters.

"Delilah and Sara are actually my half sisters," she went on. "We share the same mother, but for obvious reasons, we know we had different fathers."

Now he moved and came to sit on the edge of her chaise. His bare hand rested on her thigh and she shifted her focus to him. Those dark brows drew in and the concern on his face was obvious.

And that was why she'd fallen so fast, so hard, for him. There was more here than sex and she wondered if he could feel that same connection. Surely, he did or he wouldn't have opened up so easily to her.

"So what are you guys going to do with that information?" he asked.

"I'm not doing anything," she told him. "I've had a great life, I love Milly, and I figure if she kept all of this from us, there's a good reason. Delilah is torn, but Sara has already contacted an investigator to find her father."

"And what about your birth mother?"

Elise pulled in a breath and sighed. "She actually passed away in prison. She had a drug problem. That's why we got taken away when we were so young and then Milly had to hire someone to track us down so she could take us in."

Antonio reached for her hand and laced their fingers together, giving her a gentle squeeze for support. "So that's what had you so rattled the other day?"

She nodded and scooted over a bit to give him more room. "I just didn't know what to think or how to react. I wanted to escape and forget."

He leaned in, placing a soft kiss on her lips before easing back. Elise wanted him to say something, but she didn't know what. She also needed to know where they stood. As much as she wanted to pretend this was her life, she also had to be realistic.

"What are we doing here?" she asked before she could talk herself out of it.

The question hovered between them and Elise knew she'd just opened her heart wide, allowing something wonderful to enter or the pain to settle in. His response would only determine which one.

"We're enjoying a drink and the night."

Elise tipped her head and simply stared at him. He knew what she was referring to and she wasn't letting him get off that easy. She wasn't a clingy woman and she didn't need a man in her life to make her complete. She'd gotten along just fine this far with dating casually and staying married to her work. But Antonio was different.

Perhaps part of her felt so comfortable because he wasn't local and she'd always known in the back of her mind this would ultimately come to an end.

But she really didn't believe that. Everything inside her just had that hopeful feeling that they had met for a reason, that they had been thrown together for something bigger than just a working relationship.

Good grief. She was starting to sound like Sara.

"What do you want to be going on here?" he finally asked.

Well, damn. She hadn't expected him to turn the question back on to her. She prided herself on being honest, so now that she'd broached the topic, she had to push on through.

"In a perfect world, you wouldn't live an ocean away," she started. "We could see where this goes and we wouldn't have to worry about all the outside problems we have because we could tackle them together."

Antonio stilled and she could have sworn he was even holding his breath. Maybe they weren't on the same page or having similar thoughts. No matter if they were or weren't, she needed to know. They couldn't just ignore the fact that he would be leaving at some point.

"I do live an ocean away," he agreed. He released her hand and just laid his on top now. "I didn't come here looking for anything other than business. I didn't expect to meet someone like you, but at this point in my life, I can't focus on anything else other than my family and everything going on there."

Even though she'd assumed he'd say something

like that, the pain of the words still hit her harder than she expected. How could they have so much in such a short time and then let it all go like nothing had ever happened? She didn't work that way. Her heart wasn't wired to love and just let go.

"I wasn't looking, either," she replied. "But even you have to admit this is more than sex."

Antonio nodded. "It is, but this isn't the right time."

"Would there ever be?" she couldn't help but ask.

Antonio reached for her and palmed her cheek, his thumb slid back and forth over her skin. "I love traveling. I love meeting new people and seeing new places. That's why I'm going to step away from the restaurants. There's more for me than staying in one place, and with them wanting my role to change, to be more of a permanent fixture... I just can't be that person."

Maybe he was telling her the truth, but all she heard was that he loved his jet-setting, playboy lifestyle. The hurt that curled all around her heart was of her own doing. She'd let this go on too long, she'd opened herself up when she knew the end result.

But there had been that sliver of hope.

"You're right," she replied. "I deserve more and should be put first in any relationship."

The muscles in his jaw clenched, but he nodded. "You shouldn't settle for anything less."

Elise reached up, covering his hand with hers. "So what now?"

"I'm leaving for Tennessee the day after tomorrow. If you still want me at the gala, I did plan to be there."

The personal side of her wanted to just cut ties because prolonging this heartache would only hurt more in the long run. But the business side of her, the one that always prevailed, knew that having him at the gala would be invaluable. To have potential clients see that Angel's Share was ready to go global would only pull in more business and garner more attention.

"Of course I want you there," she told him with a smile. "I bought my dress earlier today and I'm saving a dance for you."

Antonio glanced over his shoulder to the discarded dress on the bedroom chair. "I hope not that dress."

She reached out and curled her fingers around his neck. "That dress was only for you."

Just because they were calling things off, didn't mean she couldn't enjoy the time she had left with him.

As she pulled him closer, his dark gaze dropped to her lips.

"One last time?" he asked.

She swallowed her emotions and urged him to lie

on top of her as she shifted her legs for him to settle between. "One last time," she agreed.

Antonio feathered his lips over hers and Elise savored the moment, knowing this would be their final time together. She had to lock in all of these memories to last her lifetime because there would never be anyone else like Antonio Rodriguez.

Antonio walked through the vineyard and adjusted his sunglasses.

Just that simple gesture had him thinking of all the times he'd seen Elise adjust her glasses and how damn sexy she'd looked in them.

"We also make an excellent grape juice and bottle it just for kids and that has been a top seller for us for the past ten years."

Antonio listened to the owner of Berry Farm Vineyard and was actually interested in everything the elderly man said. The history of the farm, the way they work and process, to the way they package and distribute. This was a family-run business and something he could appreciate.

But his mind was back in Kentucky, back with Elise. He'd left Benton Springs last night and had hardly slept in his hotel room. He wanted to reach out to her, to text or call or something, but he'd made it clear he wasn't in a place to move beyond physical, and staying personally connected would only confuse her and hurt her more.

And that was the part that really got him. He'd seen that hurt in her eyes when they'd been on his balcony. He knew his words had affected her, but he hadn't wanted to lie and he knew she deserved better than what he was ready to offer.

The thought of her with another man, though, that sure as hell didn't sit well with him. He already hated the faceless guy who would no doubt enter her life and make her smile, pull out that passion, have her dress in killer dresses just to take them back off.

"So what do you think?"

Antonio had to push aside his jealousy and rage and focus his attention back on the reason he was here. He smiled against the sun and slid his hands into his pockets.

"This is quite an impressive establishment," Antonio replied. "One that I think would tie nicely with the way we run our own businesses back home. I'm anxious to get to the tastings to see what we could pair with the various menu items we'll be adding."

The man smiled, causing wrinkles around his eyes to deepen. "I think we can make that happen. Right this way."

Antonio followed behind and slid his cell from his pocket. He tapped the screen, cursing beneath his breath when disappointment hit him hard. There were no messages from Elise. What had he expected? He'd called things off, though he did promise her one dance at the gala.

He was already counting down the days to get her back into his arms again. Though that was utterly foolish, he still couldn't stop himself. He also couldn't help but wonder if he'd made a mistake in ending their personal relationship. Part of him wanted to see where things went, but the other part was much more realistic. Where could they go from here? They lived on two different continents with two different lives. They both had family that depended on them.

As Antonio walked into the tasting room, he attempted to push aside his thoughts of Elise. The problem was, he didn't think he'd ever be able to get her out of his mind.

Sixteen

"This is it, ladies."

Elise glanced around the open two-story portion of the distillery. In mere moments the place would be packed...she hoped.

"I'm more nervous now than I was on our opening day," Delilah admitted.

"I was definitely more nervous then," Sara added as she smoothed her dark hair over one shoulder. "Let's do this, girls. We are about to bust onto this male-dominated scene in a bigger way than ever before."

"That's the plan," Elise said with a laugh. "Go ahead and let them in."

Delilah headed toward the double mahogany doors and cracked them open. She spoke to the employees they had on the outside to monitor the guests and make sure only those who RSVP'd were allowed in. They had security all lined up, the valet drivers, the caterers, the DJ—they were counting on this to be a huge success.

While nerves might be swirling through Elise, she also had confidence that they would no doubt make this next ten years even more impactful than the past ten years. Because this next chapter in their distillery all started with the ten-year bourbon, then the fifteen, the twenty, and they would have a continual momentum that would only propel them to greatness.

She should be thrilled that their monumental night had finally come. They'd worked toward this for so long and sacrificed so much. Hell, Delilah's marriage had fallen apart because of their dedication. Or that was what Elise assumed. Delilah never went into details.

But Elise had her own issues and her own heartache right now. As much as she loved her dress, her hair, she felt gorgeous and was ready for an epic night, she also wondered if Antonio would actually show. She hadn't spoken to him in days, not since she left his house after their last passionate night. That had been the most difficult moment, just walking away like he hadn't changed her entire world. Like he hadn't left an imprint on her heart that no one could ever fill or even come close to touching.

"Might want to smile," Sara murmured. "People are starting to come in."

Elise blinked and pulled herself back to the moment. She couldn't let anything, not even heartache, get in the way of this important night. Her sisters were counting on her.

Once the double doors were propped open, Elise recognized many people, but there were some she didn't know. She crossed the open space to start greeting her guests and thankfully, her sisters were part of this, too. There was no way she could get to everyone. They certainly had to divide and conquer.

As she shook hands and accepted congratulations from her guests, her eyes scanned the room, but she still didn't see Antonio. Maybe he'd changed his mind or maybe he'd gotten busy. If he didn't show, she had to admit that she would be even more devastated, but she had no hold over him and no control. They had a fling, or likely that was how he saw it. Whatever they had, it was over, so dwelling on what might have been or what she was missing would get her nowhere.

All she had to do was go right back to the determined, professional woman she'd been before she met Antonio. Unfortunately, she wasn't the same woman and she never would be. He'd changed her forever and quite possibly ruined her for any other man.

Elise showed guests toward the tasting area on the back wall where staff was lined up to accommodate everyone. There was also an area where they could receive information on partnering and becoming a VIP client. The key for tonight was to get everyone to fall in love with Angel's Share and if they weren't already on their customer list, to get them there.

"There's a couple looking for you."

Elise turned from the tasting area when Sara whispered in her ear.

"A couple?" Elise asked.

Sara nodded. "They're over by the waterfall."

Elise glanced toward the feature wall they'd had put in when they'd opened. They had the Angel's Share emblem etched into limestone and displayed as a thin sheet of water slid over it and into a rock base. They'd spent a good amount on this feature, but it was still one of Elise's favorites.

As she maneuvered within the crowd, she noticed a tall man with black hair and a crisp black suit, and a very petite woman with long, silky black hair. The lady had on a conservative floor-length red gown with sleeves and Elise wondered why they specifically asked to see her.

"I'm Elise," she announced as she came to stand behind them. "How can I help you?"

The couple turned from admiring the wall, and

the woman had a soft smile, while the man was the one who spoke.

But he didn't have to say a word. Elise knew exactly who they were because she could see Antonio in both of them.

"It's a pleasure to meet you." Mr. Rodriguez extended his hand. "I am Carlos Rodriguez and this is my wife, Ana. You know our son, I do believe."

Elise smiled, but the nerves in her gut swirled more than any other time in her life. She shook their hands and tried to remember they were her new customers...not the parents of the man she'd fallen so hard for.

"I had no idea you were coming," she told them. "I would have made special arrangements for you, but I'm so thrilled you're here."

"Oh, nothing special needs to be done for us." His mother waved her hand in dismissal. "We're actually here to see you."

"Me?" Now her nerves seriously kicked in to high gear. "What can I help you with?"

"It seems you've captured my son's attention," Carlos told her. "We've never known another woman to have him so..."

"Flustered," Ana finished. "I believe that's the word you're looking for."

Confused, Elise glanced around to the people milling about. Everyone seemed preoccupied with their own conversations and nobody was paying any attention to hers. Her quick scan also confirmed that Antonio still hadn't arrived.

"We mean that in a good way," Ana quickly added.

Something about her seemed so warm and welcoming. That must be where Antonio got his softer side. But when Elise looked at Carlos, she could easily see how Antonio would look in thirty years. Still handsome with that darker, mysterious air about him.

"I don't guess I know what you mean."

Elise thought she knew, but she certainly wasn't jumping to any conclusions and she was even more confused now. What had Antonio told his parents? He'd ended their personal relationship, so the fact that they had flown all this way surely meant something, but Elise had no clue what.

"Since coming here, Antonio has had a different tone in his voice when we talk on the phone. Lighter. Joyful. Our son has had a difficult time since his brother's death," Carlos offered.

"They were twins. Two peas in a pod. That's why he travels so much," Ana added. "He can still be social, still stay connected with people, but not make any lasting relationships. It's all done in the name of work. We thought when he met the right woman, he'd settle down and commit. But he pushes everything and everyone away."

Everything started to make more sense now. At

least, she thought it did. Had he pushed her away because he was afraid? Granted, their time together had been so fast, so intense, she'd been terrified of her own feelings…especially since she'd still been in the grieving process. Elise had wondered if she could trust her feelings, but there wasn't a doubt in her mind that everything she'd experienced with Antonio had been authentic and real.

"But when he talks about you, he's different. We came to find out why."

Shocked, Elise fumbled for how to respond. "He told me about Paolo," Elise finally stated. "I can't imagine the loss you all experienced. He told me you had planned for Paolo to take over the restaurants."

Carlos's dark brows shot up. "He discussed all of that with you?"

Elise nodded. "I hope that doesn't bother you. I've not told a soul and he knows he can trust me."

Carlos and Ana shot each other a look, then smiled. Clearly, they had that special bond where they could communicate without using words. Elise didn't realize she envied something so trivial until just now. She wanted that, and she knew she could have something so special and meaningful with Antonio.

"Mom. Dad. What are you doing here?"

Elise turned, her heart in her throat at the sight of Antonio behind her. His eyes went from his parents to her, then he raked that dark gaze down her dress and back up.

"I still like the other one," he told her, before stepping toward his mom and dad.

Even in the midst of his shock and surprise, Antonio still managed to slip in just enough to have her memories flooding back and remind her just how good they were together. The man was so potent and much too powerful for her to mentally ward off. She had to just stop trying because they were meant to be together. If he was afraid, then she'd help him overcome the fear.

As far as the rest of their issues, well, they'd work on that later. What was important, what she was holding on to, was the fact that his parents obviously knew something substantial for them to show up here on such an important night.

"I'll let you three talk," Elise offered.

"Stay," Antonio demanded.

Elise remained still, but she knew she shouldn't be in the middle of a family conversation, especially when she'd just met Carlos and Ana.

"Why don't I show you all to my office where you can chat in private?" Elise suggested. "And when you're done, come back and find me?"

"That would be perfect," Ana stated with a smile.

Elise motioned for them to follow her as she maneuvered through the crowd. Both Delilah and Sara caught her eye as she exited the main area and went into the hallway, which led to a back staircase to the second floor.

They reached her office and Elise punched in a code, then opened the door wide so they could go in.

"The door will lock itself when you leave," she told them. "Can you find your way back okay?"

Carlos and Ana entered, but Antonio stopped right in front of her. "I know my way."

He looked so achingly sexy in that all-black suit. She hadn't expected him to look at her the way he was now, like he was torn between what he wanted and his duty. She hadn't mentally prepared herself to see him after they broke things off, either.

But all of that would have to wait because clearly there were some family dealings to tie up and once he was free of that and her night came to an end, she had some questions herself.

Namely what he'd told his parents about her and why they were so insistent that he'd fallen for her.

Antonio reached for her hand before she could move away and leaned in to her ear. *"Asombrosa."*

She wanted to ask him what that meant, but he'd already moved away and into the room with his parents. Elise pulled the door and headed back to the gala. She had many guests to see and no doubt questions from her sisters. She'd known going in this would be a memorable night, but she hadn't realized just how much so. Now that she had a little leverage on Antonio, she wasn't going to just let this relationship go so easily.

Both her professional and personal lives were about to change forever.

Antonio slid his hands into his pockets and stared across the room. His heart beat faster than usual and there was a bundle of nerves from so many different angles. He'd start with his parents and then go see Elise and figure out what the hell was going on.

But first, he wanted to know what his parents had said to Elise before he'd arrived.

"Why didn't you tell me you guys were coming to the States?"

"We wanted to surprise you," his father told him. "And we wanted to meet Elise."

"How did you even know her name?"

His mother laughed. "There's not much we don't know about our son, but we figured the woman you'd been talking with regarding the new account was likely the same one who had you preoccupied here."

He'd never said he was preoccupied and he'd sure as hell never even acted like he was seeing anyone.

"What's this really about?" he demanded. "You don't fly this far for a surprise to talk to a woman I'm doing business with."

"But there's more than business, isn't there?" his mother asked.

Antonio crossed his arms over his chest and glanced between his mom and dad. "That's the reason you're here?"

His father took a step toward one of the leather club chairs in the seating area of the office. There were two chairs and a sofa and Carlos gestured.

"Let's have a seat and talk."

Antonio wasn't in the mood for a chat or to be checked up on, if that was what they wanted. He had a gala to get to, a sexy woman to dance with, and a final goodbye to have.

He'd made up his mind that once he left here tonight, he would be moving on to his next destination and wouldn't see Elise again. He'd gone over in his mind if he should stay the night, but they'd already agreed the other night was their last.

He just hadn't had enough of her yet…and while he'd been in Tennessee, he'd not been able to do much other than think of how Elise had flawlessly slid into his world. How, even going through her own loss and sadness, she'd talked him through his own issues.

Something had shifted inside him, something that he could only attribute to having Elise in his life. His future seemed clearer now. Everything about her seemed to fit perfectly…but nothing was perfect. Everything always came to an end…but maybe it didn't have to this time.

"We've been talking about our retirement," his

father started after they were all seated. "We know taking over our lifestyle isn't what you had in mind."

Antonio eased forward on the sofa and rested his elbows on his knees. His father sat in the chair to his right and his mother in the chair to his left. He didn't want to hurt either one of them, so he waited until they said more so he could get a good feel for exactly what they were trying to say or what their thoughts were.

"We want you to live your life," his mother told him. "When we started our first restaurant, we wanted to have something to give you and your brother. Then when he passed, you seemed to shut down. Over the years we just knew this life wasn't for you."

Antonio couldn't believe what he was hearing. Never once had they given a clue that they understood he didn't want to take over.

"We tried to push you," his mom went on. "We wanted you to love this life and we wanted to leave you a legacy. We know how much you love traveling and there's nothing wrong with that. Staying in Spain might not be for you, son."

Antonio pulled in a deep breath and tried to process what she was saying. But he knew they still wanted to keep their restaurants open and the pubs they were working toward opening.

"So what will happen with everything you have

now?" he asked. "This is still your baby. Your entire lives have been wrapped up in Rodriguez's."

His mother shot his father a glance and Antonio shifted to focus on his dad.

"We've been discussing that," his father started. "We were hoping to come to a solid compromise."

Antonio eased back on the sofa and crossed his ankle over his knee. As much as he wanted to get back downstairs, he also needed to devote his attention to this moment. He loved his parents, would do anything for them, so the fact that they could see his uncertainty without him saying a word really hit him hard. They were just as devoted to his happiness as he was to theirs.

"We'd like to still turn everything over to you." His dad held a hand up before Antonio could reply. "But as you know, we have some of the best managers and they would keep things running when you aren't around. If you want to pop in every month, every other month, whatever. You can easily keep up other ways and make sure the businesses are running smoothly and likely handle any matter from wherever you are in the world."

The suggestion seemed so easy, so perfect for their situation. Could the solution be so clear? Would everyone be happy with this and could they all actually pull it off?

"I don't want to let either of you down," he told

them after a moment. "I wanted to find a way to tell you, but at the same time, part of me wondered if I should just take over and let you all go live your lives. You've worked so hard for years."

"And so have you," his mom countered, reaching to place her hand on his knee. "Without you, one of us would have had to have traveled all over and taken care of getting new and unique things for our restaurants. Without you, we wouldn't be nearly as successful as we are today. So you are certainly no disappointment."

Hearing her say that instantly pulled a weight from his shoulders.

"You flew all the way here to tell me this?" he laughed. "A phone call would have worked just fine."

His mom patted his leg. "Yes, well, I tried calling the other night, remember? When you didn't return my call, I thought I'd try reaching out again."

Oh yeah. He remembered. That night was seared into his mind forever.

"I have to assume you've been a little sidetracked by a beautiful distiller," his mother went on.

Antonio didn't deny the claim, there was no reason to. "She's special."

"I'm thrilled to hear that." His mother beamed. "Perhaps she will be good for you in more than just business."

Oh, she would be, but he wanted to talk to Elise

about everything before he fully opened up to his parents. Suddenly, the pieces of his chaotic life seemed to be falling exactly where they belonged.

Seventeen

"What is going on?" Sara whispered as soon as there was a slight lull in the crowd.

Elise waved to a familiar client who had just entered the room. "Antonio's parents surprised him."

"Don't you mean surprised *you*?" Sara asked.

Elise nodded. "That, too."

"What did they want?"

"They're either checking me out or discussing Antonio's role in the family business," Elise stated under her breath. "Probably both, but we'll have to talk later. I'll fill you and Dee in once we close out the night."

Elise followed Sara through the crowd, barely

even hearing the music that played at the other end of the room. People were taking advantage of the dance floor and enjoying the classics that Delilah had requested.

And speaking of Delilah, Elise hadn't seen her sister since she'd come back from upstairs. Maybe she was with a VIP client or perhaps she was assisting a staff member.

Several members of the Angel's Share family all worked the crowd, passing out tiny tumblers with sample pours of their first ten-year bourbon. For those non-bourbon lovers, there was also gin. Anything to get new clients or show their current clientele just how epic Angel's Share spirits were. They were unlike any other, especially in this bourbon country territory.

Elise spotted Camden out of the corner of her eye. He came from one of the back rooms that were only for employees.

Camden's eyes locked on to Elise and she smiled and offered a wave. No matter what was going on between him and her sister, Elise did think of him as a brother.

"Well, all of the Hawthorne ladies look absolutely stunning tonight." Camden leaned in and kissed Elise on the cheek before turning and doing the same to Sara. "This looks like a successful night. Your hard work and dedication really shows and this turnout is great. Milly would be proud."

There came that burn in the back of Elise's throat

that she didn't want to happen while surrounded by shrouds of people, especially on what should be one of the happiest days of her life.

"Don't get us crying," Sara scolded. "We all had our makeup professionally done and we look damn good."

Camden laughed and nodded. "That you do," he agreed. "I won't stay long and I know things are strained, but that doesn't mean I didn't want to show my support."

Elise spotted Delilah off in the distance, talking to some guests. Dee's eyes kept darting in their direction and Elise knew having Camden here was difficult.

"You talked to Delilah?" Elise asked, already knowing the answer.

Camden's smile faltered. "We talked, yes."

"Is that all?" Sara asked, which earned an elbow from Elise.

Camden shook his head as he blew out a sigh. "Chemistry doesn't change anything, though. Chemistry was never our problem."

Elise couldn't help but think of her relationship with Antonio. Their chemistry definitely wasn't an issue. The completely different lives, homes, and baggage they each had was.

Still, she couldn't ignore all that worked for them, and all that they'd already shared in such a short time. With such a tight bond between them, Elise couldn't even imagine how amazing a future would be. But she had to talk to him, she had to see where his head space was because she didn't believe for a minute that he truly wanted to push her away. Going back to life before Antonio didn't even seem possible.

"I won't pry," Elise told her still-brother-in-law. "But I'm rooting for the two of you."

A sadness overcame his eyes and he leaned in to give her a hug, then did the same to Sara. "I'm going to head out. Congratulations again."

As he walked away, Sara moved in closer to Elise's side and sighed.

"He's hurting as much as Delilah is."

"And they're both stubborn or something is seriously wrong that she won't talk about," Elise murmured. "But we can't fix anything right now and we still have a couple hours left, so let's focus on this."

Because this moment was all she could concentrate on. They'd worked too damn hard to let anything else interfere with this night. And once this was over, she had to shift to her personal life and make the biggest decision she'd ever made with her heart.

The time had come to lay it all on the line.

Antonio waited until the gala was over. He waited even longer until he knew Elise would be home. He hadn't had to do much digging to find her address and he had to admit, the grounds were amazing. She lived up on a hill and her home was nestled back against the woods. A large pond sat off to the left of her two-story brick house. There was a large side porch that faced the pond and an instant image of the two of them enjoying morning coffee hit him hard.

Even though it was late, her porch lights illuminated the side of the house, the front of the house, and there were lights on inside. She was home and all he had to do was get out and knock on her door. All he had to do to change their lives was tell her everything he'd been mulling over since speaking with his parents.

But would Elise be up for what he had to say? Would she even want to hear his ideas? He'd broken things off and then he'd vanished from her gala. He hadn't seen her since she showed him into her office. He'd had good reasons, but would she understand?

Antonio had never allowed fear or uncertainty to hold him back from anything in his life, but right now he wasn't so sure he could step from his car and walk those few feet to her porch.

Just as he shut off his engine, Elise's front door swung open and she appeared. She still had on the silky green gown, the one that reminded him of satin sheets and how perfect she would be to unwrap. His eyes met hers through the windshield and she remained framed in the doorway with the lights from inside illuminating her. She just stood there, waiting on him, and he knew this was his chance. All he had to do was take it.

He opened his car door and stepped out, then rounded the hood and met her gaze once again.

"My driveway alarm went off ten minutes ago," she told him, still in the doorway. "Were you thinking of leaving?"

"More like thinking of what the hell I was doing."

She crossed her arms and tipped her head with that smile of hers that never failed to punch him right in the gut. She had a power over him, a power no one had ever had before. He never thought he'd like giving up control of any aspect of his life, but he'd quickly discovered there were worse things… like being without the one person who filled a void.

"And did you come to a conclusion?" she asked.

"I did."

He started toward the base of the porch, then stopped. With his hand resting on the railing, he propped his foot on the bottom step. He'd rehearsed his speech in his head on the drive over here, but now that he was in the moment, all of those perfectly placed words failed him and he had nothing. All he could think was how stunning she was, how she'd slid right into his life when he'd needed her most, and where the hell they'd go from here.

"Before you say a word, I want to say something." Elise took a step to the edge of the porch and looked down at him. "I'm not sure why you didn't come back to the gala. I assume you were with your parents and I completely get that. They are lovely people, by the way."

He couldn't help but smile, and he would have told her exactly what they thought of her, but she plowed right on through.

"I know we have totally different lives," she went on. "I mean, we don't even live on the same continent, but I'm overlooking that for now."

She gathered the side of her dress in her hands and came down one step, then stopped.

"I mean, how can we just ignore all of this attraction and chemistry?" she added. "And I'm well aware that relationships aren't based solely on those things, but it's a hell of a start and we pretty much excel at chemistry."

Down another step.

"And I know you wanted to end things and I almost let you—"

He laughed, unable to help himself. "Let me?"

"I figured you knew what you were talking about and that you didn't feel the same way I did. But your parents changed everything."

Down another step. They were only two away now. Still too damn far.

"They said you push every type of commitment away since your brother died. I never thought of that, but it makes sense. With you not wanting to take over their chain, all the traveling you do to keep busy and moving, and then us."

Down one more. She dropped the material of her dress and looked into his eyes.

"There is an us," she insisted. "You might not want to look at our situation that way. You might believe this is all still a fling or I'm just someone you passed the time with, but—"

Antonio framed her face and covered her mouth with his. He couldn't stand not touching her another second and he never, ever wanted her to believe that she was just a fling. That couldn't be further from the truth.

Elise grabbed hold of his shoulders, her fingertips curling in as she held on. There was something so damn soothing about being with her. He still couldn't put his finger on it or even try to label it, but...

Wait. Yes. He could label this.

Antonio eased back, still holding on to her face. "You weren't someone I was just passing the time with. And if you're done talking, I have a few things to say myself," he demanded.

"Am I going to like this?" she asked.

"Depends on how you feel about splitting your time between here and Spain."

Her eyes widened, her mouth dropped to a perfect O and he wanted nothing more than to kiss her again, but he had to keep going.

"I have a solution for us."

"Us?" she whispered, her face still full of shock.

He tucked her hair behind her ears and trailed his fingertips down her jawline. "Us, just like you said, remember?"

"I didn't think you thought we could be one unit," she admitted.

"I didn't," he confessed. "I had no clue how I could have you, have a life that still made my parents proud, and try to figure out what to do with their businesses. Because at the end of all of this, I guess I want my twin to be proud of me, too. Paolo is still such a huge part of my life."

"And are you clear now of what you want?" she asked.

Antonio settled his hands on her hips and placed a kiss on her forehead before focusing back on his speech and her expressive eyes.

"I know that I want to take a leap and commit my heart to someone." He leaned in closer, close enough to feel her warm breath falling on his lips. "And I want to take that leap with you."

"Wait...what?"

"You heard me. I want to take the leap with you," he repeated. "My parents' restaurants and new pubs will all be in my name. I will need to go every now and then to check in, but I can also run things from anywhere in the world since we have trustworthy managers on-site."

Elise blinked. "Wait."

"You said that already."

She closed her eyes, shook her head, then looked back to him. "You mean you want to make this work between us? I had all of my bullet points rehearsed and I was ready to tick off each box to you to prove why we should make this work. The only thing I didn't know how to solve was your parents' business."

His heart opened and he realized that this wasn't painful or scary at all. The only emotions he felt were elation and love.

"Te amo."

A wide smile spread across her face. "I'm going to need to learn Spanish."

"I love you," he repeated in English.

Her eyes filled with tears. "Are you serious?"

"I've never been more serious."

A tear slipped out and trailed down her creamy skin.

"Te amo," she told him.

Antonio bent down and lifted her into his arms. Elise looped her arms around his neck and rested her head against his shoulder as he headed toward the still-open front door.

"You're learning already," he told her. "And by the way, my parents want us to come to breakfast so they can welcome you into the family."

"Breakfast? I'd love to."

With the heel of his foot, he closed the door and

glanced around the foyer. "Now, lead me to your bedroom because I have plans for you until we have to meet up with them."

Elise's lips pressed against the side of his neck. "Up the stairs. Last door on the left. And you still owe me that promised dance."

He carried her up the steps and to her room, what would be their room, because he wasn't going anywhere for a while. He would do whatever it took to keep them together because nobody had ever captured his heart, his whole life, the way this woman had. He would give up anything for her, but thankfully, he wouldn't have to. He could still carry the legacy of his family and finally work on settling down with the perfect woman.

"Tell me you love me again," she murmured as he stepped into her bedroom.

"*Te amo*. Always."

* * * * *

Don't miss Delilah's story,
Second Chance Vows
Available Fall 2022!

WE HOPE YOU ENJOYED
THIS BOOK FROM

✦ HARLEQUIN
DESIRE

*Luxury, scandal, desire—welcome to
the lives of the American elite.*

Be transported to the worlds of oil barons, family dynasties,
moguls and celebrities. Get ready for juicy plot twists,
delicious sensuality and intriguing scandal.

6 NEW BOOKS AVAILABLE EVERY MONTH!

SPECIAL EXCERPT FROM

◆ HARLEQUIN

DESIRE

Finding his father's assistant at an underground fight club, playboy Mason Kane realizes he isn't the only one leading a double life. So he offers Charlotte Westbrook a whirlwind Riviera fling to help her loosen up, but it could cost her job and her heart...

Read on for a sneak peek at
Secret Lives After Hours
by Cynthia St. Aubin

They stood facing each other, the summer heat still radiating up from the sidewalk, the sultry breath of a coming storm sifting through their hair.

Now.

Now was the moment where she would pull out her phone, bring up the ride app. Bid him good-night. If she did this, the past three hours could be bundled into a box neither of them would ever have to open again. He might smile at her secretively every now and then, wink at her in acknowledgment, but that would be the end of it.

If she left now.

"Come up," Mason said.

It wasn't a question. It wasn't even an invitation.

It was an answer.

An answer to her own admission in the elevator. That she liked looking at him. That she could look at him more if she wanted.

That he wanted her to.

"Okay," Charlotte said.

Don't miss what happens next in…
Secret Lives After Hours *by Cynthia St. Aubin,*
the next book in The Kane Heirs series!
Available August 2022 wherever
Harlequin Desire books and ebooks are sold.

Harlequin.com